BLUE BLOOD

A JOHN JORDAN MYSTERY THRILLER BOOK 20

MICHAEL LISTER

PULPWOOD PRESS

Paperback ISBN: 978-1-947606-33-3

For Dave Lloyd

My brother and best friend.
My life was greatly enhanced by your presence in it. My life
has been greatly diminished by your absence from it.
I miss you everyday.
Every. Single. Day.

THANK YOU

Thank you Dawn Lister, Michael Connelly, Aaron Bearden, Mike Harrison, Tim Flanagan, D.P. Lyle, Micah Lister, Meleah Lister Smith, Dave Lloyd, and Jill Mueller for your support and assistance with this work.

BLUE BLOOD

1

"I'm not trying to be a martyr," Malia Goodman says. "I'd much rather live for the cause than die for it."

Author and activist Malia Goodman is a forty-something African-American woman with cinnamon skin so flawless it looks to have been airbrushed on by a skilled and careful artist who takes great pride in his work.

She is tall and athletic and attractive—exceptionally so, though her allure is as much the result of her bearing and her bruised soul as her big, bright, black eyes and the features of her heart-shaped face.

Merrill and I are in her hotel room at the Holiday Inn on MLK across from the mall in Panama City. Her handler, Rodney Livingston, a tall, bony, older black man, and her assistant, Tana Kay, a small, pale, plain-looking black woman in her late twenties, are also present.

The remodeled room is light and airy—a stark contrast to the dark, dramatic, Victorian whorehouse-looking decor with blood-red drapes it had once flaunted.

"I'm not particularly brave or heroic," she says.

She is both, and it speaks well of her that her self-deprecation seems genuine.

A social justice activist specializing in police-civilian relations and a *New York Times* bestselling author of books on the same subject, she is in a particularly poignant and unique position to speak about policing procedures and the criminal justice system.

Her new book, *Shots Fired*, is an in-depth look at police and policing techniques, including a look at the alarming number of shootings of unarmed citizens by law enforcement.

On an extended book tour that involves marches, protests, and rallies, she typically stays anywhere from two days to two weeks in each city she visits and attempts to expose injustice while there. Two police shootings—one out in Panama City Beach and one in Downtown Panama City—have brought her to town.

Though not officially associated with any other groups or movements, Malia's work often parallels and occasionally intersects them.

"Don't get me wrong, there are days when joining

Graham and Malik is far more appealing than anything this world has to offer, but . . . I'm enough of a coward to want to die peacefully in my sleep of old age."

In separate and unrelated incidents, both Malia's husband, Graham, and her son, Malik, had been shot and killed.

Graham Goodman had been a detective with the LAPD who was killed in the line of duty by a drug dealer high on bath salts as he was attempted to question about the death of his girlfriend. Malik Jackson, an up-and-coming young rapper and aspiring actor, had been gunned down by police during a routine traffic stop. Malik, who was unarmed and happened to be black, was shot and killed by a white cop. Graham, who was a highly respected and decorated cop who happened to be white, was shot and killed by a black drug dealer.

At times Malia's writings and speeches sound like she's the staunchest defender and apologist for law enforcement. At others she sounds like the angry mother of an unarmed son who was executed by those very same police. The truth is she is both, with both supporters and detractors on both sides—and recently someone from the second group has made both threats and attempts on her life.

That's why we're here. Well, that's why Merrill is here. He's interviewing to provide security for her while she's in the area for a series of speeches, protests, and book signings. I'm here because I'm on administrative leave and not in a good way, and Merrill has been taking every chance he can to get me out of the house and away from the alcohol and self-loathing I have stockpiled there.

"Anyway . . ." Malia says to Merrill. "You look like you'd be good for the job. Hell, you look like you could stop a scud missile, let alone a crazy with a gun, but . . . well . . . would you? Would you really put yourself in harm's way to protect me?"

Merrill nods, but doesn't say anything.

"That's it?" she says. "That's all I get? *A nod*?"

"I can verbalize it if you like," he says.

"I would like."

"I would," he says.

"Why?" she asks, trying to suppress an amused smile.

"Because I said I would," he says.

She nods as if she understands. "You'll risk your life to keep your word," she says.

He nods.

She waits for him to elaborate but he doesn't, and there is an awkward silence.

Like the colorful carpeted hallway, the room smells of commercial cleaning products and an air freshener questioning its identity. Does it want to be citrus or floral? It has so far been unable to decide.

"Your code includes death before dishonor?" she asks.

"That's not the way I would put it, but . . . something like that."

"And that's it?"

He shakes his head.

"Then what else?" she asks.

"In your case," he says, "there's more to it than just my word."

"Like what? Do you mind explaining it to me?"

"If I said I'd protect a white supremacist, I would," he says. "Even if it costs me my life to do it. But with you . . . Let's just say your views are far more in line with mine than a white supremacist's would be."

"All my views?" she asks.

"Most of them."

"On both sides of the issue—my support and defense of cops and my calls for reforms that would keep unarmed citizens from getting killed?"

He nods. "Some of my best friends are cops."

She gives him a radiant smile and something passes between them—something indefinable that includes both appreciation and attraction.

"*And*," Merrill adds, "though I am rarely unarmed, *I am* a black man."

"So you'll protect me more than you would the white supremacists?"

He shakes his head. "The same. I was just trying to

reassure you, let you know what my answer to Marley's question is."

"Which question is that?"

"How long will they kill our prophets while we stand aside and look?"

She is visibly moved that he regards her as one of our social prophets.

"And your answer is?" she asks, her voice thick with emotion.

"No longer."

She nods. "You're hired. Rodney will handle all the details. I've got a conference call I need to be on, but you're most certainly hired. And I'd like you to start as soon as possible."

Merrill nods.

When Malia stands, Tana and Rodney jump to their feet as well. Merrill and I also stand—just not as quickly or enthusiastically.

Malia shakes Merrill's hand and then mine, and then Rodney leads us out of her room. Before the door closes, she and Tana are already going over the talking points for the conference call.

As soon as Malia's hotel door is closed behind us, Rodney's demeanor changes. "Okay," he says, "now that we've got that out of the way we can have the real interview. And I'd really like to meet with Merrill alone."

Merrill starts to protest, but I cut him off.

"Sure," I say. "I have somewhere I need to be anyway."

"Cool," Rodney says. "It's nothing personal, just . . . you know."

"Don't go far," Merrill says. "I'll hit you up soon as I'm done."

While Merrill meets with Rodney in his room upstairs, I meet with Merrick McKnight downstairs in the bar.

Like the rest of the hotel, the bar has been remodeled. It's lighter and brighter and more open.

I liked it better before.

Merrick and I were meant to get together later in the evening, but when I called him and told him my schedule had unexpectedly freed up sooner than I had thought it would, he said he was both close by and available to meet now.

"Cheers," I say, holding up my vodka and cranberry.

"Cheers," he says, clinking his bottle of Bud Light against my glass.

We both sip our drinks as an uncomfortable silence creeps in around us.

Merrick had asked to meet with me and had not said why, so I drink as I wait for him to introduce a topic of conversation, glancing occasionally at the basketball game on the muted TV monitor mounted above the bar.

It's my first drink of the day and it's all a first drink should be.

"I've never seen you drink before," Merrick says.

"Is that why things just got awkward?"

He shakes his head. "Well, maybe," he says. "But if it is, it's only part of the reason. The biggest is what I need to talk to you about."

I nod and wait and drink.

Near the open entrance of the bar, beyond which the mostly empty lobby can be seen, a balding black man with a too thick beard softly plays a grand piano.

"There're actually two things I wanted to talk to you about," he says.

"Is one any easier than the other?" I ask.

He nods. "A little."

"Well, why not start with it?"

He nods again, takes a long pull on his Bud and sits the bottle on the beige bar top in front of him.

"I'm worried about you," he says. "We all are."

I nod again slowly and say, "I can see why you would be and I appreciate it."

"That's not the first thing I wanted to talk to you about but it sort of sets it up," he says.

I take another drink.

A loud burst of laughter erupts from the lobby as three inebriated women in their late twenties pitch forward through the sliding glass doors, holding on to each other for support.

Please don't come into the bar. Please don't come into the bar. Please don't—

"*Oooh*, piano," one of them says. "Let's go into the bar. Let's 'o to . . . bar. Come on. Just one 'ore 'ittle drink."

"*Tiff*," one of her friends says with great emphasis, "*you promised*. Nightcap in the room then straight to bed."

"Er'ry par'y has a pooper an' at this par'y . . . and at 'is . . . You are it. *Hey, Mr. Pia'o Man*."

Her voice grows even louder and the piano player stops mid-note on the chorus of "Walking in Memphis" and starts playing Billy Joel's "Piano Man."

The abrupt transition into the new tune is lost on Tiff.

"Hey, Mr. Piano Man," she says again. "My lame friends're makin' me go up 'o 'ed. See you 'nother time for some tic . . . tickle . . . ticklin' 'ose ivories."

The three young women stumble out of view and eventually out of earshot.

"How are you?" Merrick asks.

"I thought we just covered that. Probably about how I seem," I say.

He frowns. "Sorry to hear that."

He pauses a moment and looks around the bar. I follow his gaze.

Besides us, there are only five other people in the spacious bar—the bartender, the piano player, a middle-aged man in a business suit at the other end of the bar, and a couple at a table in the far back corner whispering intimately between kissing intensely.

"You've always been there for me," he says. "Always so understanding and accepting and positive. I really appreciate the way you've always been with me and my kids."

The bartender looks down our way and asks if we're ready for another yet. Merrick shakes his head though his bottle is almost empty, so I assume he's only having one.

"Thing is . . ." he continues, "you do so much for so many . . . I wanna make sure somebody is doing something for you. I wish I could, but . . . I'm no counselor or sponsor or whatever, but . . . I know someone who is. A friend of mine happens to be a really great counselor. You two have a lot in common. I've often thought—even before . . . now . . .before what you're dealing with—that I should introduce you two because I know you'll hit it off. He works out of the country and is only here for a few weeks every three months. I've told him about you and . . . I think it'd really do you good to talk to him."

"Thank you," I say. "That means a lot. I really appreciate you thinking about me."

The pianist is now playing a rousing rendition of "Sweet Caroline," really banging the *bamp bamp bams*.

"Will you talk to him?" he asks.

I start to shrug, but stop.

"As a favor to me," he adds. "Will you? Please."

I nod.

"You will?"

I nod again. "I will."

"Ah man, you don't know how happy that makes me," he says. "How relieved it makes me feel."

His genuine delight at my willingness to talk to his friend on top of the kindness he is showing me stings my eyes and makes my throat constrict. I glance away, blinking and trying hard to swallow.

When I am able to look back at him, I say, "That was the easier of the two things you needed to talk to me about?"

He nods and smiles, but the smile quickly fades into a frown.

"No easy way to say it," he says. "So I guess I'll just . . . Reggie and I broke up."

"*Really*?"

I'm completely caught off guard. Based on the occasional offhanded comment made by Reggie, I guess I've known they've had issues—but what couple doesn't? I never suspected anything like this, had no idea they had already pronounced time of death.

"She hasn't said anything to you?" he asks.

I shake my head.

"That's so like her," he says. "Probably part of the reason we broke up—she buries most everything. Not really willing to talk about much of anything."

"I'm so sorry to hear that y'all are—"

"It's been comin' a while. Everything started so good between us—so damn good. Best ever, but then . . . I don't know . . . our differences started showing more, became more pronounced. We drifted apart. Started arguing more. And no matter what I tried she . . . she just wasn't willing to talk about it. It's so funny . . . you think it'll be the big things—somebody having an affair or going through some sort of crisis or you'll have some big issue related to sex or kids or money, but . . . and then it's just a million little things. You get so far apart you can't figure out how to get back together—or why you ever were in the first place."

"I really hate to hear that," I say. "How are you doing with it? You okay?"

"I'm okay. I really am. Like I said it's been a long time coming. I mean, I hate it, but . . . I'm okay. It wasn't all of a sudden like someone dying or something. It didn't catch either of us by surprise."

"Well, it certainly has me," I say.

"I wanted to talk to you because I knew I'd be seeing

you less and I wanted you to know and to keep an eye on Reggie—to help her if she'll let you."

"Of course," I say. "I'll look out for her."

"I know you're going through your own shit right now."

"That's the best thing for it," I say. "Get out of my own cycle of self-pity by helping someone else. But I'll still see you."

"I'm actually moving over here," he says. "Casey already attends college and works over here and there's a good school for Kevin. I can't make a living as a journalist in Wewa. I've taken a job with the *News Herald*. I'm sure our paths will still cross occasionally but probably not nearly as often. That's why I wanted to go ahead and tell you in person—that and to introduce you to Dave."

"Dave?"

"My counselor friend I was telling you about."

"Oh. Gotcha."

"You up for meeting him tonight?" he asks.

"Maybe not tonight, but soon," I say.

"I just feel like if you don't meet him tonight you might not ever. Please. Just for a few minutes."

3

"Now, look, my young brother," Rodney says when he and Merrill are in his room. "I'm glad you made a love connection or whatever that was with Malia. She needs to be comfortable with who's gonna be guarding her. But I gotta know you can do the job and that you're really worth the money. I'm the one bankrolling this operation. I'm the one calling the shots."

Merrill doesn't say anything.

"Oh, you a hard nigga, that it?" Rodney says. "Well, I guess that's good when you protecting the princess, but . . . you ain't gonna get the chance to do that, you don't convince me you the right man for the job."

Though Rodney's room is nearly identical to Malia's, something indefinable about it makes it seem like it's not as nice. It's not as bright and well lit. It doesn't smell as good. And it's not as fresh and clean. But Merrill decides the real difference is the absence of Malia herself.

"Thought I already had the job," Merrill says. "Ain't tryin' to be hard. Just listening to you and tryin' to get the lay of the land. Didn't realize Ms. Goodman wasn't in charge."

"Oh, she thinks she is," Rodney says. "And I'm happy for her to think that. She's very good at what she does. Makin' a real difference, but she's naive. The threats are real—from a lot of different directions. She wouldn't last a day out here on her own."

As Rodney talks, Merrill gets a good look at him for the first time. He's a tall, thin, older man in a cheap burgundy suit with long hands and bony fingers. His eyelids are loose and droopy and appear hooded. Peeking out from behind them, his small, watery eyes are wary and furtive.

"Maybe I'm a bad judge of character," Merrill says, "but she doesn't strike me as naive, and I'd say given what she's gone through, what she goes through every day, she's tough enough to handle most anything comes her way."

"I'm not sayin' she's not tough or strong, not resilient in a certain way," Rodney says, "just that she's . . . She's a . . . a visionary I guess you'd say. She's a big-picture type of person, not good with details. That's all.

I'm not saying anything bad about her. Just letting you know—"

"Who calls the shots," Merrill offers.

Rodney leans back and studies him for a long moment before speaking. "You fuckin' with me, boy?"

Merrill's brow furrows as he looks up and squints, seeming to consider something.

"You have to think about it?" Rodney asks.

"About what?"

"Whether you're fuckin' with me or not."

Merrill shakes his head. "No, not that."

"Then what?"

"I's tryin' to remember that last time I's called *boy*. And what I did to the man who said it."

Rodney holds up his elongated hands, palms out, in a placating gesture. "Didn't mean it like that. Sorry. Got caught up in playin' the old man role a little too much. Tell you what . . . you let that one go and I'll let the fact that you were fuckin' with me go."

"The only reason I'm still here," Merrill says, "only reason I haven't knocked you on your old black ass, is how much I respect the lady and admire what she's doing and know I can protect her better than anybody else. But there are limits even given all that and we've about reached 'em. Hire me or don't, but get on with it."

"You should be the best for what you charge," Rodney says. "You come highly recommended by the right people, but goddamn you're pricey. I could hire three bodyguards for what I'd be payin' you."

"Get what you pay for," he says. "And you ain't just gettin' me. But I'm willing to give Ms. Goodman a discount for the cause."

"That's very generous of you and would be greatly appreciated. Thank you. But we've got to talk about who'd be helpin' you. The gentleman who came with you tonight isn't right for what we need."

"I say who's right to work for me and nobody's righter than John."

"Righter or whiter?" he asks. "And it ain't just that he's white. He's a cop."

"Two things Ms. Goodman obviously doesn't have an issue with."

"As I said she can be too naive for her own damn good sometimes," Rodney says. "The thing is . . . this isn't just about who can do the job but how they look doing it. I've got to consider the optics involved in everything we do."

Merrill turns without a word and leaves the room.

Rodney follows him.

Merrill steps down the hallway and knocks on Malia's door.

"Wait," Rodney says. "There's no need for . . . Don't disturb her. We can work this out."

Tana opens the door.

"Did you make sure it was us?" Merrill asks.

"No, I'm sorry, I just . . ."

"I need to speak to Malia a moment."

"She's—"

Malia appears behind her. "What is it?"

"Just came to say goodbye and to make sure you knew why I wasn't taking the job," he says.

"I thought you already had," she says.

"I did too, but evidently, Rot-ney here calls all the shots because he's bankrolling this little operation and he thinks I'm too expensive—even with my offer of a discount because I believe in what you're doing—and my friend is too white and too much a cop to be working for you. It was an honor to meet you. Keep up the good work. And maybe be a little more selective about who you surround yourself with."

With that, Merrill nods to her and turns to leave.

"Wait," she says. "Please."

4

"We can make it very difficult for someone to kill you," Merrill is saying to Malia, "but we can't make it impossible. If a madman with a gun or a bomb or even a knife is committed enough he'll eventually get close enough."

"Unless you stop him before he does," Malia says.

Merrill nods. "Unless that. And that's what I intend to do. But I just want you to know the reality of the—"

"I do," she says. "I know absolute safety like absolute certainty is an illusion and unattainable. I also know the reality of Rodney's situation. Hopefully he won't be a problem, but if he is, you let me know. I can't do everything, so I have to delegate, but if there's ever an issue I need to step in and fix it. Fast. What we're doing is too important not to."

"Let's talk logistics," Merrill says.

"Let's do," she says. "Tana, can you step over for this?"

Tana, who has been on her phone and a laptop on the other side of the room, stops what she's doing and walks over to where we are standing near the door.

"Tana is my right hand," Malia says. "We're virtually inseparable. She needs to hear everything we're saying about how this will all work."

Tana Kay, Malia's intern-secretary-travel companion-assistant-surrogate daughter, is a thin, young, plain-looking light-skinned black woman in her late twenties. She is quiet and shy and seems perpetually ill at ease. She is bright and bookish, but behind her small, unfashionable glasses she blinks a lot and often looks both wary and afraid.

"Since things got off on the wrong foot with Rodney," Malia says, "let's start by going over what everyone does. Rodney does call most of the day-to-day, moment-to-moment shots, but not because he's in charge. I've made him my operational manager. And he does a lot. But he works for me. He's very protective and mostly means well, but he has a tendency to overstep his boundaries. Usually, he's quick to make a course correction when I point something out, but . . . we're in some uncharted waters right now. Though he works for me and I pay him a salary, he recently loaned me—or more precisely our operation—some money. It's just until I can finish my next book and get the rest of the advance for it and can do a little more fundraising—both of which take time that I'm spending in other ways just now. It's very expensive to do what we do and I'd have to do less of it in order to fundraise or write more books and . . . anyway, Rodney offered the loan and I took him up on it. It may have been a mistake. But that's probably why he feels even more emboldened lately. He normally doesn't travel with us, but he insisted on coming with us this trip. Anyway, that's all things for me to deal with but I wanted to give you some background so you know what you're walking into. As far as Tana . . . she's my heart and soul. Couldn't function without her. But sadly I'm going to have to pretty soon. She's planning to leave me at the end of next month. She helps me with everything. She's far more than an assistant. She helps with my writings and speeches and appointments and keeps me sane. If you have a question and I'm not around or available, ask her."

Tana gives a quick, awkward smile and a little nod.

Merrill nods and says, "Got it."

"Okay," Malia says. "Logistics."

"We'll need to know more about the threats to evaluate the potential risks and come up with a comprehensive strategy," Merrill says, "but in general, one or both of us will be with you at all times while you're here. And we may have to bring in additional help. If we do, it will only be one or two others and they will be people I trust."

"That's fine and it makes me feel safer already," she says, "but we've got to weigh risk versus reward. I can't be hindered from what I'm doing. And I can't appear to be afraid—though, to be honest, sometimes I am. And as a woman, I can't be seen to be this helpless little thing unable to carry out my mission without a man to protect poor little ol' me."

Merrill nods. "We'll be in the background. And we'll stay there until we're forced into the foreground by a threat."

"Even then I have to insist on measured responses," she says. "I'm out here as a force for justice and equanimity opposing unnecessary violence. Nothing to do with my organization can even appear to employ tactics we oppose. I know I'm putting you in a very difficult position, but . . ."

Merrill shakes his head. "We get it. Won't be a problem."

"*We?*" she asks, glancing over at me. "Does Silent Bob over there ever say anything?"

"I've been known to," I say.

"Well, it's good to know you can anyway," she says. "'Case you need to tell me to duck or some shit like that."

"Some might even say I'm *well spoken*," I say with a smile.

Her face lights up, and I can tell she instantly gets my

riff on the racist compliment black people, especially those in public life, so often receive.

She looks at Merrill. "He's a keeper. I like him. Well .. . I'm sure there's more we need to cover, but I'm hungry and tired and still have calls to make and emails to respond to. Can we pick this back up in the morning?"

"Sure," Merrill says.

"And when we do," Tana says, "we need to talk about the attempts on Malia's life. Because all I've heard y'all mention so far are threats, but there've been a lot more than just threats."

5

"You sure you don't mind meeting like this?" I ask.

"Not at all," Dave says. "I'm happy to. I've conducted counseling sessions in far stranger places."

Dave Lloyd is a large, laidback man with coarse gray hair and glasses in his mid-fifties. He has a relaxed, accepting manner that makes him easy to talk to. A licensed mental health counselor with over twenty-five years' experience, Dave was raised in Panama City but has lived and traveled all over the world. Because of his travel schedule, Dave's private counseling practice is mostly done online these days.

He and I are seated in padded conference room chairs at the end of the third-floor hallway not far from Malia's room.

Since I'm not sleeping much these days anyway, I offered to take the first shift, and Merrill took me up on it, saying he didn't want to take the chance of having any other dealings with Rodney Livingston tonight.

When Merrick had explained to Dave where I would be and what I would be doing tonight, he had offered to come by after his gig at the Little Village in St. Andrews. In addition to being a licensed mental health counselor, Dave is a musician and singer who performs at several restaurants and bars both in Panama City and on Panama City Beach when he's home.

Like me, Dave has a background in theological studies, and I'm surprised our paths haven't crossed before now.

"How do you know Merrick?" I ask.

"He's attended a lot of my gigs over the years, and has written a few pieces for the paper here and there—a profile on a band I was in, a feature on a food program I was involved with. I don't know . . . seems like I've always known him. How about you?"

"Met him when I moved to Wewa," I say. "He used to date my boss."

"He told me he and Reggie broke up," Dave says. "I was very sorry to hear that."

I remind myself again to call and check on Reggie.

The hallway is dim and quiet and seems to extend into an infinite horizon.

It's a strange place to spend prolonged time in, and it reminds me of a story Daniel Davis told me about having a panic attack in a hallway while standing guard outside the room of his future wife Sam Michaels back when they first met. They were hunting a serial killer who used fire as a weapon, which brought them to interview the Phoenix at PCI where I was a chaplain at the time, though we didn't actually meet until a few years later.

Dave and I continue small talk for a while that isn't small talk at all. I can tell he's letting me get comfortable with him, and it's working. Over the course of unhurried conversation and unawkward silences, we eventually arrive at the real reason he's here.

"I just feel so guilty," I say. "And I don't just mean about what I did—that in itself is nearly debilitating— but if I ever catch myself not feeling guilty, not thinking about what I did, I feel guilty about that. I walk around with this oppressive heaviness that is weighing me down and causing everything else to fade into the distance— every experience is muted, every feeling subdued. I feel disconnected from everything."

"I'm so sorry to hear that, man," he says. "It sounds like in addition to the guilt and everything else . . . you're still in shock."

"I have a real hard time eating anything," I say, "but when I do—no matter what I eat—nothing has any taste. It's . . . just all so bizarre—like I'm trapped deep inside this body, observing everything from a great distance, not experiencing anything directly."

He nods his understanding and expresses his empathy but doesn't say anything.

"It'd be one thing if it were just me," I say, "but I have a wife and two daughters, other family and friends who count on me . . . If it were just me . . . I might be able to walk around like a soulless . . . But with my girls, I can't keep . . . I feel so guilty that I'm not giving them what they need, that I'm not really with them even when I am."

"So much guilt," he says. "Coming at you from so many directions."

It's late and we've been talking for a while, and our throats are tired, our mouths dry.

"None of it unwarranted," I say.

"Well . . ." he says, "just because there are reasons doesn't mean it's warranted. Even beginning with the initial incident . . . As I understand it—and not just from you, but Merrick and others—it was an accident. And not just an accident but . . . you were set up."

Dave's compassion is palpable and I find just being in his presence therapeutic and buoying.

"And on a certain intellectual level I know that is somewhat true," I say, "but that does nothing for how I'm feeling. Nothing at all."

He nods. "You can't think your way out of this, and knowing something on an intellectual level isn't the same as experiencing it on an emotional level, but . . . every single feeling we have is preceded by a thought. Your thoughts are causing you to feel what you're feeling."

I think about that.

"So, mindful practices to help you deal with your thoughts would be very helpful and a great starting place," he says, "but let's go back to the guilt itself for a moment. You said none of your guilt was unwarranted. Is that true? Think about how we respond to things that happen. Sometimes we respond appropriately but others we either over or under respond. Certain guilt we feel is proportional. We failed a friend or lost our temper or said something unkind and we feel guilty. But other forms of guilt are disproportional. We take too much on ourselves —too much responsibility for the actions of others. I think it would be worth your time to explore whether the guilt you're feeling—especially as it relates to what happened in that school hallway that day—is actually proportional. You strike me as the kind of person who is constantly trying to help others, which is . . . heroic, but often people like that take on the weight of and responsibility for those others. If you're prone to do that, then your guilt response is likely to be disproportional."

He's right, of course, at least about the type of person I am and my approach to life and other people.

"You don't ask others to be responsible for you, do you?"

I shake my head.

"Earlier you mentioned you were drinking again," he says. "Is Anna responsible for that? Johanna? Anyone other than you?"

"Absolutely not."

"You take responsibility for what you do. Shouldn't you let others do the same? As I understand it the actions of others played a far, far greater role in what happened than the actions you took. If that's true, are you still taking sole responsibility for everything? Are you taking the guilt and responsibility that is rightly theirs?"

"It would certainly be pretty to think so," I say.

6

I crawl into the hotel bed bleary-eyed and raw-boned weary but not particularly sleepy.

It's early, so I call Reggie first in case Anna's not up yet.

Merrill and I are sharing a room right across the hall from Malia's so we can sleep in shifts and be close by when we're needed. Between ours, Malia's, Tana's, and Rodney's, we have the last four rooms at the end of the northeast corner of the third floor.

"Morning," Reggie says.

"Morning," I say.

"You're up early for a man of leisure."

"Actually, just turning in," I say. "But I wanted to call and see how you're doing first."

"Merrick talked to you, didn't he?" she says.

"Yeah."

She doesn't say anything, but her breathing changes.

Our room has two double beds in it. Next to mine, Merrill's is made and appears not to have been used, though I know he slept in it last night.

I hope he doesn't expect me to make mine when I stumble out of it in a couple of hours to meet with Tana to do the threat assessment.

"How are you?" I ask.

"Not great," she says.

"I'm really sorry," I say. "I thought you two were . . . good together. Thought you really made the opposites attract thing work like a mofo."

"Yeah, me too. I mean . . . I knew we had some issues . . . and I guess I knew he wasn't as happy as when we first got together, but . . . I don't know. As much as I figured going in that something like this would eventually happen . . . it still caught me by surprise."

"I wish you would've let me know," I say.

"You've been dealing with plenty of your own problems."

"Doesn't matter," I say. "I feel bad that you didn't think you could talk to me about it."

"It wasn't that I didn't think I could. Wasn't that I didn't want to. I just . . . I usually shut down. Handle shit like this on my own. And I didn't want to be a bother when you were dealing with so much—first with Chris, then the shooting at Potter High."

"Still," I say.

"I know."

"I mean it."

"I know."

"I'm here," I say. "Call me when you need to talk. Anna too. And come to dinner soon."

"I'm bad company right now, but—"

"So am I," I say. "But Anna can handle both of us."

She laughs. "I'm sure she can. Sounds good. Just need a little longer to . . . But I will."

"Good."

"You 'bout ready to come back to work?" she asks.

"Soon," I say. "Sort of had in mind to come back after I finish giving my deposition."

"Well, do what you got to," she says. "Get better. Deal with your shit. But then get your ass back here. We miss you. Got a case we could really use you on too."

"I will," I say.

She doesn't say anything for a beat and I wait.

"Thanks for calling, John," she says. "Thanks for caring about this ol' cowgirl."

"I do," I say. "And don't you forget it. Call me sometime soon just to hear me say it."

After Reggie and I end our call, I take a moment and

attempt to do one of the mindfulness exercises Dave suggested I try before calling Anna.

The exercise doesn't go well, and I wonder if it's the fatigue or something else—like my general state of mind even after a rare good night's sleep.

I think about how problematic it is that it's my troubled mind that I have to rely upon to deal with my troubled mind. Ironically, my mind is meant to be both the disease and the cure.

Giving up on mindfulness for the moment, I call Anna.

"Hey," I say.

"Hey," she says.

Her voice is soft and sleepy, unbearably sweet and sexy.

"I miss you so much," she says. "Can't stand sleeping without you."

"Same here," I say. "Only more so."

"It's not a competition, John," she says playfully. "But I miss you more."

I laugh. "Not possible."

Neither of us says anything for a moment, and I think about how very much I like listening to her breathe.

Even over the phone her presence is palpable, her love and camaraderie nourishing.

"Merrick came by to see me last night," I say.

"Over there?"

"Yeah. He's working at the *News Herald* now."

"Oh?"

"He and Reggie broke up," I say. "He and the kids are moving over here."

"Oh no," she says. "I . . . I don't know quite what to say . . . It's like I'm shocked but I'm not really all that surprised. It's hard to explain. I hate it for all of them. Gonna miss having him and the kids around. Have you spoken to Reggie?"

"Just a few minutes ago."

"You called her first?" she says in mock reproof.

"Only to let you sleep a little longer."

"How is she?"

"Same as him. Sad. Hurt. At a loss."

"Any idea what happened, why they're ending it?"

"Don't think it's just one thing," I say. "Don't think it's something dramatic or . . . Not like an affair or a betrayal of some kind."

I pause but she doesn't say anything.

"How does it make you feel?" I ask.

"Sad."

"How does it make you feel about us?" I ask.

"I'm not sure I follow."

"Does it make you feel more vulnerable? More susceptible? Like our relationship—all relationships are fragile? Precarious? Uncertain?"

"Not in the least," she says.

"Really?"

"Really."

I pause and before I say anything else she speaks again.

"Does it make you feel those things?" she asks.

"Not in terms of how I feel about you or my love for and commitment to you, but . . . in terms of . . . I guess I was already thinking you might be . . ."

"Be what?"

"Given the state I'm in," I say. "Given the fact that I'm drinking again."

"What, you thought I might be having second thoughts or—"

"Something like that," I say.

"*John*," she says. "Of course not. Absolutely positively, 100 percent not."

"So that's a no?" I ask.

"You're the man of my dreams," she says. "The best man I know. My heart breaks for you and what you're going through right now but it only makes me love you more, want you more, want to care for you more."

Unable to stop myself, I break down and begin to cry —though quietly enough so that she is able to keep talking.

"And as far as drinking," she says, "I know why you want and need to stop—so that you're not actively addicted to anything, so that nothing has that kind of control over you. And I get it. But it's not as though you become a different person when you drink. You're still my sweet John. You're still my hero, still all I want in the world. I know you want to get active in recovery again and I want that for you—but only so you can be fully present in your life, not altered or preoccupied or controlled. I wouldn't love or want you any less if you never stopped drinking again. So with all you're going through or dealing with, mark worrying about me or us off your list. Okay? I know I've gone on and on but I want to make sure you understand. Wild horses couldn't drag me away."

e don't want any trouble," a thin, elderly man blinking behind his big glasses is saying. "Not if we can avoid it."

"You already have trouble," Malia says.

"You know what he means," an overweight woman in a white dress and huge hat says. "We're not going to be party to picking fights, stirring up . . . stuff."

Malia is meeting with the African-American Ministerial Action Committee of Bay County about her planned protests and rallies in a small, dingy fellowship hall of a church on 11th Street a few blocks off MLK.

Merrill, who had driven her over, stands in the back of the room, observing the proceedings. Rodney, who was supposed to be with them, had canceled at the last minute. Merrill wasn't unappreciative.

It's the little things, he thinks.

The African-American Ministerial Action Committee of Bay County consists of—at least as it is constituted here today—less than a dozen ministers, mostly middle-aged men and women, representing as many churches across the area. Each member present only speaks for his or her congregation and, like membership in the group, participation in its sponsored activities is strictly voluntary.

Malia is here today to discuss the committee's involvement in her social justice activities while she's in town and address any concerns they may have.

Turns out they may have a lot of them.

"Peaceful protests, a march for civility, and a rally for justice are the opposite of wanting trouble, picking fights, or stirring things up," she says.

The hard-surfaced hall looks to have been built and decorated in the '70s. Dusty, faded, earth-tone curtains hang limply in front of too small windows, and the dull cement floor is finished with speckles of brown, orange, and gold.

"But the response . . ." adds a chubby young man with a soft voice and hands to match. "Think of Charlottesville. We are peaceful, but between the counter-protesters and police presence . . . things always get out of hand and *we* are always the ones who wind up getting hurt or killed."

"First," Malia says, "things don't always get out of hand. I've been involved in hundreds of protests around the country without a single incident, but what others do —how they respond, the tactics they employ, any hate and violence they perpetrate—is no reason for us not to calmly and peacefully bring attention to injustice, to stand together and speak out against it."

The central air-conditioning cycles on and the fellowship hall is filled with an airy swishing sound and the faint smell of insecticide.

"It's risky," a thin middle-aged man with a large afro who looks like a skinny Don King says, "and I'm not sure it's worth it. What good does it really do?"

Malia takes in a deep breath, holds it, and slowly releases it. Merrill can tell she's trying to contain her frustration.

"It does a lot of good," she says. "A lot. Putting positivity into the world always has a positive impact. It shows that a group of people are united in a righteous cause and are comporting themselves with dignity and civility—and the more people there are, the bigger message it sends to those in power, those making decisions about law enforcement and social justice issues and governance. That's why we need all of your congregations to participate. We need numbers."

"I don't know," a middle-aged woman in a mint green dress says, shaking her head. "Seems to me . . . more numbers means more chances for things to get out of hand . . . for somebody to get hurt or killed. Numbers seems like it has more to do with the ego of the organizer than anything else."

"Panama City is a small town," Malia says. "Even if everyone you represent participates it will still be a relatively small march and rally. I'm not here for ego or numbers. I could be a hundred other places for that. I'm here because we have an opportunity. That's all. That's all it is. An opportunity to lift a voice, shine a light, be a witness. I didn't organize any of this. It's not *my* march or *my* rally. It's—"

"But you will be the face of it," Mint Green Dress says. "Moment you arrived you became the face of everything that happens here."

"I 'spect so," she says. "But I'm going to participate whether there are any cameras pointed at me or not, because it's the right thing to do given the opportunity we have."

"I'm just not convinced," Skinny Don King says. "There are complexities and subtleties to our situation here that—"

A tall, handsome man who looks like a young Denzel Washington in a clerical collar stands, the sound of his chair sliding back drawing everyone's attention and silencing Skinny Don King.

"I'd like to make a motion that we remove the word

action from our name," he says. "It's hypocritical to have it in there. We can take it out or just replace it with *inaction*. Whichever this esteemed body deems best."

A small smile twitches across Merrill's lips.

"I keep imagining if Dr. King were in this meeting," he continues. "I'm sure he was in many just like this—where good-meaning people were afraid of taking on the injustice of the status quo, as bad as it was, because they believed it could always get worse and knew it probably would before it got better. Or small-minded people who didn't want to march with him because they knew he, as the face of the movement, would get all the credit. Those people who didn't take the opportunity they had been given were on the wrong side of history. Just as we will be if we don't take a stand, find a voice, walk a little mile together for peace and justice. Ms. Malia, I and my congregation will be there to march with you and it will be our great honor to do so."

"Thank you," she says.

"Now, I'm gonna go before I say anything else, but before I do, you need anything else from me or have any questions for me?"

"Just two quick questions," Malia says. "Are you single and do you like older women?"

8

"She's far more afraid than she lets on," Tana Kay is saying. "And she should be. There are some truly sick individuals who wish her ill."

While Merrill is with Malia at a ministerial meeting at a church on 11th Street, Tana is going over the threats and attempts with me.

Because I didn't want to meet with her alone in her room, we are in a small seating area off the right side of the lobby, the large, oblong coffee table before us filled with notes, letters, cards, and packages—all of which threaten Malia in some way.

The indoor pool is behind a frosted glass panel wall to our right, the faint smell of chlorine mixed in with all the other competing aromas layered into the huge lobby.

To our left the wall holds a variety of appreciation plaques from Tyndall Air Force Base, many of them made to look like partial airplane wings.

I woke after a few hours of sleep with the Rolling Stones' "Wild Horses" in my head and the assurance of Anna's love in my heart. Between the wise, caring counsel I had received from Dave Lloyd and the absolute and unconditional love I had received from Anna, I felt if not a faint, remote hope, at least the possibility of it.

"It speaks to how scared she is that she hired Mr. Monroe to protect her," Tana is saying. "For a while she just dismissed the threats as bored crazies with nothing better to do. And I'm sure a lot of it is exactly that. Probably all the online expressions of hate are. But for someone to take the time to create an elaborate and detailed threat and find out where you are and hand deliver it to you there . . . that's another level. Between those and the actual attempts on her life, she finally started taking them seriously."

The plan is for me to investigate the threats against and attacks on Malia when I'm not helping Merrill guard her.

"Malia mentioned you're leaving your position at the end of next month," I say. "Is that because of the threats?"

"It's a lot of things. Mostly because I want to spend more time writing and reporting. I do a lot of writing for

Malia, but I have to do a lot of administrative and secretarial duties too. I don't want my writing to suffer because I'm constantly putting out little fires for her—responding to emails, drafting speeches, answering calls. But . . . if I'm completely honest . . . I'm sure the danger has something to do with it too. But it's not just that. It's the workload. All I do is work. Because of Malia's disability nearly every task takes a lot, lot longer."

"Disability?"

"Oh, well . . I really shouldn't say anything because it's not public knowledge, but . . . Please don't say anything. She finds it embarrassing—though she shouldn't. She suffers from dyslexia."

"I see how that would make your job a lot harder."

Across the way, the lobby looks like a million others in the world. Three people are in line at the front desk. A loaded luggage cart stands unattended near the sliding glass front doors. The tables of the restaurant are set and ready. Traveling sales reps or consultants in business attire come and go—along with the occasional Air Force or Navy officer in uniform. All to the sounds of cable news from the TV mounted near the main seating area, the dings of the elevators, the quiet conversations of business people whose temporary home this is, and the mechanical, rubbery sliding sound of the opening and closing of the glass doors.

"Do you already have another job lined up?" I ask.

She shrugs and shakes her head. "Sort of . . ." she says. "Because I've been traveling and working nonstop for Malia I haven't had time to spend any money, so I've got some saved up. My plan is to just write and see if I can get another book contract and maybe start speaking some. The truth is I have a book of my own already finished. It's a critique of social justice movements—Black Lives Matter, Me Too, Occupy Wall Street, things like that. For this next release with Malia I'm going from uncredited ghostwriter to credited co-writer. That should open some doors for me. Malia's going to blurb my book and maybe even write an introduction for it. We'll see. The thing is . . . there's no question I'd have more opportunities and a much larger audience if I stay with her—I could speak to and write for far more people—but . . . Malia casts a big shadow and I just don't think I can continue to grow and evolve as a person or a writer in the shade of that shadow."

"So you're leavin' 'cause Malia's throwin' shade?" I say. She laughs a little.

"Does she have a replacement for you yet?"

She shakes her head. "I think she's in denial. Hoping I'll change my mind and stay. She's dangled all sorts of carrots in front of me. But the other reason . . . and I know this is going to sound terrible, but . . . I'm going to be very difficult to replace in terms of all the various things I do.

She can find someone to write her speeches and books but not be her travel companion and surrogate daughter and receptionist and media specialist and secretary and counselor and so on. I've told her she should break the responsibilities up into different jobs and hire three people instead of one. My guess is she thinks that if she doesn't hire someone I'll stay a little longer and . . . she's probably right."

"What would happen to the organization and or the movement—if I can call it that—if something happened to Malia?"

It's an indelicate question but I'm using it to gauge Tana's reaction and attachment to Malia.

"Well . . ." she begins slowly, "a martyr is a truly powerful thing. Rodney has mentioned wanting to continue the work and maybe even have me take up her mantle but . . . I don't know. I'm a writer. Not really a speaker. I don't know . . . But let's prevent that from ever being an issue."

She looks at all the hate spread out on the table as she says this, and I follow her gaze.

"Take me through them," I say.

"I've divided them up into various groups," she says, pointing to the rows. "There are two broad categories—those pro-police and those anti-police. There are people in each group that criticize and condemn her. It's funny because their letters just say the exact opposite things—

things that can't both be true. The way we tend to see things from our own little perspective is astonishing. You never can please everyone so might as well not try. Within those two main categories we have a lot of subcategories—including those with misogynistic rhetoric and those with racist rhetoric. I'm telling you she gets it from every conceivable angle. Under the racial category she has white people saying *die nigger die* and black people saying she's sold her race out and that she's not really black. In the misogyny camp you've got men threatening to rape and defile her for the filthy whore she is and others saying she must have a dick because there's no way she's a woman."

"What about obsessive fans?" I ask. "Do you have a folder for them?"

She shakes her head. "No, but I could make one. She has plenty of super fans. I'm one of 'em."

"I'm talking about the kind that have tried to insert themselves into her life and that she's had to reject," I say. "The kind that feel like they know her and she should be their girlfriend or best friend or help them get their book published or help make them famous. Things like that."

She nods. "I'll pull those together for you."

"Do all the letters and notes and things here contain overt threats?" I ask.

"Yes. I only included the ones that have serious

threats in them. The ones with mild criticisms or corrections or rebukes would fill this room."

"Have you separated out the ones that contact her over and over?" I ask.

She nods. "That's what most of these are."

"If you put aside all the critics and all the crazies who've sent a single letter . . . and just went with those who are relentless and obsessive and actually have shown up in person—maybe even more than once . . . who would you say feels like the biggest threat?"

"There's a wounded ex-cop who runs a racist website," she says. "The grieving, unhinged dad whose little girl was shot by police. The crazy rightwing nut who blames Malia for the cancelation of his radio talk show. He makes podcasts and YouTube videos now and shows up places to harass her. I'm sure you'll meet him. Hell, you'll probably meet all of these nutters before it's over. The only other one, and the only woman, is a lady who does what Malia does—speaks and writes books—but she's very extreme and no matter what she tries she can't get any traction. She labors in obscurity and blames Malia for taking up all the oxygen on these issues."

"Well, I'll start with them while I look through the rest of these. Thanks for organizing all of this for me. Malia is very lucky to have you working with her."

"It's an important cause and I'm lucky to be contributing to it."

I glance out into the lobby and see Rodney leaving the hotel with an athletic forty-something white man in a trim-cut suit.

"Tell me about the altercations she's been involved in," I say. "Has she been physically attacked? Have there been actual assassination attempts?"

She nods. "We've all been involved in little skirmishes with counter-protesters or aggressive police officers. I'm not including anything like that. Now, she doesn't agree that all of these were personal attacks on her or attempts on her life, but I think they are. I think there have been attempts in Atlanta, Chicago, and Madison, Wisconsin so far. She was run off the road outside of Madison. A truck T-boned her and rolled her car into a lake. She thinks it was just a hit-and-run accident, but I don't and neither do the police. One night after a rally in Atlanta we were walking a couple of blocks to this all-night diner and we were shot at. She says it was more likely a random drive-by than an attempt on her life, but it wasn't. In Chicago, a guy broke into her hotel room and assaulted her. He broke in through the sliding glass doors from the balcony and attacked her with a knife. She was able to fight him off and get away. He dropped his knife on his way out. It was the biggest hunting knife I've ever seen. Was wicked. She says it could just be a rapist breaking into a random room, not a crazy trying to kill her specifically, but he didn't try to rape her. He didn't try to steal anything. He just tried to kill her. I think there are others, but I'm certain about these."

She hands me a file folder that wasn't with the others on the table.

"Here're the police reports and the investigators' names and contact information. You don't have to take my word for it. Ask them about it."

9

W hen Merrill checks the church parking lot there is no one in it, but before he and Malia can reach the rental car, four men rush them.

Two middle-aged, two twenty-somethings. All white. All muscular. All enraged.

One of the middle-aged men, the leader, has a bat in his hand. Merrill recognizes him from the news coverage of the Antwone Wright case and thinks his name is Louden. He's the father of Boyd Calhoun, one of the Panama City Beach cops accused of killing the unarmed Antwone.

Merrill isn't sure whether Boyd is in custody or not but he's not among the men coming at them now.

"You niggers think you're gonna come into our town

and get my boy strung up you got another thing comin','"
Louden says.

Before he can raise his bat, Merrill snaps out a hard
right jab to his throat.

As he drops the bat and grabs his throat wheezing,
Merrill comes out with a .45 from beneath his coat and
puts himself between Malia and the men.

Without looking or saying a word, Merrill wraps his
free arm around Malia and backs her toward the car.

After helping Louden up and giving him back his bat,
the four men close in on and encircle Merrill and Malia.

The traffic on 11th is slow and steady but no one
seems to notice the assault happening in the side parking
lot of the African Methodist Episcopal church.

"You gonna shoot us now, you cocksucker?" the taller
of the two younger guys says. Like the others, he bears a
distinct family resemblance to Louden. Probably a
brother or cousin to Boyd.

"Not unless you force me to," Merrill says, his voice
calm and quietly menacing. "How 'bout y'all walk away
while you still can."

"There's four of us, you dumb son of a bitch," the
shorter young man says.

"All that means is I'll have four rounds left over and'll
have to find four other racist assholes to shoot. And
dumb is bringing a bat and four guys to a gunfight with
one of me."

Louden, still rubbing this throat from where Merrill punched him in it finally has his voice back. "We just came to talk."

"Your bat says otherwise," Merrill says.

Louden looks down and seems surprised to see that bat back in his hand.

"It's a bad neighborhood," the tall young guy says.

Young Denzel runs from behind the building, his phone held out videoing as he does. He comes up beside the group and makes sure the four men see him recording.

Merrill can hear Malia let out a little moan and clear her throat behind him.

"Y'all need to turn around and go home," Young Denzel says.

"Not 'til I say what I came to," Louden says through his hoarse throat.

"Then take a step or two back and say it," Merrill says. "Then get the fuck outta here."

Glancing over at the phone recording them, the four men take a few small steps back. As they do, something seems to soften a little in Louden.

"My boy's a good man," Louden says, his voice more sad than angry now. "He's got a family, kids. He's a good man and a good cop. He'd never shoot an unarmed kid. Never."

"Well, in fact, that's exactly what he did," Malia says,

taking a step out from behind Merrill. "He shot and killed an unarmed kid in his own backyard, and if he's as good a man as you say, he'd acknowledge the terrible tragedy and horrible mistake for what it was and ask for forgiveness from Antwone's family instead of trying to make it out to be Antwone's fault somehow. I'm sick to fuckin' death of the blame-the-victim game."

"That's not what he's doing," he says. "Y'all just want blood. You're here to make sure he gets strung up. You don't care that he's a good man. All you want is his blood —and some free publicity."

"It's funny how you keep using the phrase *strung up*," Malia says, "because the one thing you don't have to worry about is your son being lynched. That's not a part of y'all's history."

"Okay," Merrill says, "you've said what you came to say. Time to go."

"I'm not done," Louden says.

"Yes you are," Merrill says.

"Please think about what you're doing," Louden says to Malia. "Let the justice system run its course without y'all stirring everybody up. Please. Don't take my boy."

"Antwone's grandmother would've said the same thing to your son if she'd been given the chance."

"You fuckin' cunt," the shorter of the young men says. "Don't you dare—"

"Tim, that's enough," Louden says. "Let's go. We've said what we came to say."

"Dumb monkeys are too dumb to understand anything any—" Tim is saying when Merrill slaps him hard across the face with his open hand.

The blow slings Tim's head to the right, a string of blood-tinged spit flying out of his mouth before his head snaps back.

"Time to go, *Tim*," Merrill says.

Rubbing the fiery red handprint on his left cheek, Tim says, "If you didn't have that gun . . . I'd . . ."

"You'd what?" Merrill asks, handing his weapon to Malia. "You'd what?"

"I'd teach you some goddamn respect."

"Well, I guess school's in, 'cause I don't have my gun anymore. Get on with your lesson then."

Tim doesn't move, doesn't speak, and he looks like he's going to wet his pants.

"I'm waiting," Merrill says. "Teach me about respect. Does it involve showing up with a baseball bat and threatening a lady? Does it include calling us niggers and monkeys and her a cunt? Oh wait, I think I may be 'bout to catch on. Is it that you can say and do anything you want to and we just have to stand here and take it? That how we show you respect, *Tim*?"

Tim remains frozen.

"He was wrong to slap you," Malia says, stepping

forward. "He shouldn't have done that no matter what you said or how much you deserved it. Ignorance and fear and hate can't be beaten out of someone. He works for me, and as his employer I apologize for him slapping you." She looks at Louden still holding his throat. "In your case I think his action was purely self-defense, so I'm not going to apologize for that. But I will tell you that my only wish is for your son to get a fair trial. I want justice for him as much as I do for Antwone. Nothing more but certainly nothing less."

"How about Carmen Sykes?" the tall young man says. "You want justice for him too?"

"I do," she says.

Without saying a word, Louden gives her the slightest of nods and turns and walks away, dragging his bat on the oil-stain-spotted cement beside him as he does.

A moment later the others follow.

Malia gives Merrill his gun back and says, "You and I need to have a little talk about how quickly this thing comes out and about not bitch-slapping little men no matter how much they may deserve it."

"Everybody wantin' to teach me something today," he says, slipping the .45 back into its shoulder holster beneath his jacket.

"And you . . ." she says, turning to Young Denzel, "thank you for joining in and for filming it. If I give you my number will you text it to me then delete it?"

"I'll text it to you and then delete the video, but not your number," he says. "Because the answers are *yes* and *yes.*"

"I'm afraid you've—"

He flashes his million-dollar smile and says, "I *am* single and I *do* like older women."

10

"I know you can't know for sure," I say to Malia, "but do you have a sense of whether the attacks have been the work of one person or different people?"

"Which attacks?" she asks.

"Madison, Atlanta, and Chicago," I say.

It's just the two of us. We're seated in a booth at The Place on Harrison in Downtown Panama City having a late lunch together. She's having the Jenks—an enormous bacon cheeseburger with onion rings and french fries. I'm having a french dip and side salad.

To hide her dyslexia, she had asked me and the waitress strategic questions, claiming to have forgotten her reading glasses.

Merrill is meeting with another client of his and I have no idea where Tana and Rodney are.

"Oh, well, I'm not even sure they were personal attacks on me," she says. "I know that's what Rodney and Tana think, but . . ."

The Place is a restaurant, bar, and live music venue in a long and narrow old building close to the Martin Theater and the Visual Arts Center. Bottlenecking in the center at the bar that divides dining in the front from the small stage, dance floor, and scattered tables in the back, the Place actually feels like two different places. Lighted liquor signs and beer advertisements hang from a green-tinted faux copper ceiling above a ceramic tile floor, and muted TVs airing sports and news shows line one wall.

"If they *were* personal attacks on you," I say. "If they're related to the threats you get because of the work you do. Same guy? Different people?"

She looks up, closes her eyes, takes a deep breath and lets it out slowly. "If I just go on my gut," she says, "let everything else go—including the fact that I'm not sure that anyone would really think I matter enough to make a run at—I'd say that Chicago and Madison could be personal and the work of the same guy. I still think Atlanta was random and had nothing to do with us."

I nod and take another bite of my french dip.

"Don't think for one moment I'm embarrassed to be eating more than you," she says. "Food is one of the few pleasures I have these days, so . . ."

She takes another big bite of her burger and chases it with a ketchup-covered wedge of steak fry.

It's midafternoon. The lunch crowd is long gone. An elderly couple on the opposite end of the restaurant are the only other customers in the joint.

"This is the best burger I've had in quite a while," she says. "Thanks for bringing me here."

"My pleasure."

"Even if it was to pump me for information."

"I'd much rather catch the guy than try to stop him the next time he strikes."

"If there is a guy," she says.

"Based on what Tana showed me, I'd say there is."

She nods. "The Madison thing comes the closest to convincing me."

"Why's that?"

"The guy who hit me . . . he wasn't coming from a side road or something. It wasn't an accident. He laid in wait and rammed me into that freezing lake. Left me there to die. There was no one else around, so either he was some sort of serial killer who uses his truck to kill random drivers on dark icy roads at night or he was after me specifically."

"And Chicago?" I say. "Gun to your head, same guy or different?"

She stops eating and focuses.

"I'm not sure why and I haven't really thought about it before but . . . gun to my head, gut feeling . . . same guy."

I nod.

"Which is strange because I had no contact with him the first time," she says. "He was inside a two-ton truck and blindsided me out of nowhere. Happened so fast. Had no interaction with him whatsoever, but something about the two attacks . . . feels the same."

"But not Atlanta?" I say.

She shrugs. "I'm not saying it's not. Just that it doesn't feel the same. I think we just happened to be close to a drive-by or some random kid just shooting in the night. If it was the same guy he's insidiously clever."

"That's what concerns me," I say.

"That was three very different attacks—three different weapons, three different towns, three very different modus operandi."

"Exactly," I say.

I can see the reality of the situation registering on her. "Well . . . hell."

"There's more," I say.

"More?"

"In among all the other threats you've received I found three very specific notes that correspond with these three attacks."

"Really?"

I nod.

Through the plate glass windows in the front I can see the slow-moving traffic on Harrison and pedestrians passing by on the sidewalks on either side. I can see them but not hear them. The only desultory sounds in the Place come from the kitchen and a satellite music station dedicated to '70s and '80s hits. Dr. Hook's "When You're in Love with a Beautiful Woman" is on at the moment.

"Are you sure? I mean positive?" she asks. "Tana and Rodney haven't mentioned anything about that."

"They didn't put them together," I say. "The threat and the attack happened at such different times and the messages were so subtle that they didn't connect them. Maybe if they had gone back and looked at them following the attacks like I did . . . but . . . Y'all stay busy and always keep moving forward."

"That we do," she says. "And that's on me. But I still find it hard to believe that all three of us missed it. Are you sure that—"

"Each threat was on a postcard from the city where it happened," I say. "In fact, they're really the same card— just with a different city. They all say *Greetings from* in cursive and have images from the city inside big bubble letters spelling the name of the city. *Greetings from Madison, Wisconsin. Greetings from Atlanta, Georgia. Greetings from Chicago, Illinois.* And they're all vintage postcards— like genuinely old. Collectible. And he must have mailed them in an envelope to preserve them because there is no postage or postmarks on them. They all have a typed note on them that alludes to the manner in which he was going to kill you."

"Oh my God," she says.

I wipe the au jus from my fingertips and pull up the pictures of the postcards on my phone.

"There's probably nothing left of any forensic value on them—if there ever was—but I've sent the postcards to the Florida Department of Law Enforcement lab for processing. Here are pictures of them."

I hold up my phone and swipe from picture to picture for her to see.

Once she has seen all of them, I pull the phone back over in front of me and read the messages.

"'An icy watery grave awaits you in Wisconsin. Stay away or wind up sleeping with the fishes. A cap awaits your ass in the ATL. Bang Bang! Your big black ass be chalked on dem downtown streets. You will die in your sleep or at least in your bed in Chicago. With my dick and my blade inside your whore ass.'"

"It's one thing to want to kill me," she says. "It's another to call my ass big. Why add insult to serious bodily injury?"

She tries to be brave and funny but can't quite pull it off, her voice quavering by the end.

"You okay?" I ask.

She shakes her head and blinks back tears. "It's just so

vicious and personal and he actually attempted to carry out his threat in all three places. It all just got a lot more real. And damn him, he's got me crying like a fucking baby. If you tell anyone, he won't have to kill me 'cause I'll die of shame."

"Your secret is safe with me," I say.

I give her another moment before I say anything else.

"I've been thinking a lot about this guy," I say. "His actions show a level of sophistication that is alarming. He's careful and patient. I'd say he's older and wealthy. He has the time and the means to travel to the towns you're in. And he didn't panic when he failed each time. He took the loss and left. Lived to fight another day. The fact that he's sending vintage postcards says a lot about him—especially since he's typing on them and doing what he can to keep them pristine. And I'd say the language he uses on them is intentionally ignorant and blunt and street—in an attempt at subterfuge."

"So you're saying he's even scarier and more resourceful than I first thought," she says. "No way I'm getting out of this alive. No way."

11

"Had the two shootings here in Panama City happened and had you said anything about coming here prior to these other attacks?" I ask.

She looks up and twists her lips.

"I'd have to give that some thought," she says. "And probably talk with Tana. I mean, obviously the Antwone Wright killing had already happened—that was over a year ago—but I'm not sure about Carmen Sykes. It's so much more recent."

I nod and think about it.

We are the only two patrons in the Place now. We've finished eating and our plates have been cleared. Besides quietly refilling our glasses the waitress is leaving us alone to talk.

"You think what's happening is related to one of them?" she asks.

"Wondering if it could be," I say. "Especially after what happened this morning. We know Boyd Calhoun's family poses a threat. Just trying to figure out if it's related or unrelated to the other attempts. We've got to be ready for it and deal with it either way, but it'd be helpful to know which it is."

She nods. "Was there a Panama City postcard with a threat on it in with the others?"

"Tana didn't give me anything received since you've been here," I say. "Only the older threats. And I didn't come across the postcards and see the pattern until I was looking over everything by myself later. But we need to look at what has come in since you've been here."

"There's usually a lag of a few days when I go somewhere new," she says. "For the first few days, the mail only comes to our office and has to be forwarded to us, but after I've been at a place for a little while, people find out where I'm staying and begin to mail or deliver things directly."

"I'll get with Tana as soon as we get back and see what else has come in."

"Thank you so much," she says. "I feel like you're going way above and beyond security services and I really appreciate it."

"Happy to do it," I say. "I'd much rather catch the guy

before he can try again than try to protect you from his next attempt. Be better for us to knock on his door than him on ours."

Her eyes moisten and she blinks several times. "The fact that you called it *our* door is . . . It means more to me than you can ever know."

"Well, that's what it is," I say. "Let's go over the two cases here—your opinions about them, the statements you've made about them. That sort of thing."

"Sure," she says. "Mind if we take a little walk while we do it? I know it'll mean you'll have to be more . . . that it'll be a bigger challenge to guard me, but I just feel as if I'm spending my entire life indoors these days."

We pay and then walk out the back door after I've checked out the area.

Crossing the mostly empty parking lot, we go behind the Martin Theater, cross 6th Street, and take Harrison down toward the marina.

The late April day is warm and clear and sunny, and reveals the subtle beauty of downtown. Being out in it is worth the extra effort involved in keeping her safe.

I haven't worn a holster with a weapon in it for over a week and wouldn't be now if I weren't solely responsible for Malia's safety. At least it's my personal gun—a slim series Taurus 9mm—and not the one I used in the Potter High School shooting. As awkward as my own weapon feels, the one I used to kill a kid feels unbearable.

Once known as Floriopolis, Harrison, and Park Resort, Panama City became Panama City in 1906—so named during a period of interest in the Panama Canal by a developer named George Mortimer West. He planned to increase real estate development in Bay County and claimed a straight line between Chicago and the capital of the Central American country of Panama intersected the North Florida Panhandle town.

Native Americans have been in the area for at least the past 13,000 years, and when the first people arrived here, the sea level was still nearly 100 feet below current levels, the Gulf shoreline some 15 miles farther south. At that time the bay was largely high and dry with the Econfina Creek creating a valley that ran down to the Gulf, the coastal forests and embayments from that period now submerged offshore, the interior river valleys from then flooded to create the depths of St. Andrews Bay.

During the Civil War, Panama City became a strategic supplier of salt to the Confederate troops, which made it a target of the Union. Over the years numerous raids were carried out, and in 1863 the town was destroyed.

Throughout its history, the port of Panama City has been a vital part of the city's development, but this was never truer than during World War II when Panama City became a shipbuilding and industrial center for the war effort.

During the war and for a time following it, Panama

City was a destination city, but within a few decades it was Panama City Beach that became the place to visit.

"What do you know about the two shootings?" she asks.

"Some, but it'd help me to hear how you summarize them, so pretend as though I haven't heard anything about them."

"Sure, okay," she says. "Mind if we walk over there?"

She's pointing toward McKenzie Park. We cross Harrison and enter the park by the fountain next to the old Sherman Arcade Building.

For a few minutes, we stroll along the brick paths beneath the shade of the massive, ancient oak trees, but eventually take a seat on one of the benches near the smaller fountain at the park's center.

"The first shooting took place on Panama City Beach," she says. "Over a year ago now. Panama City Beach Police Department gets a call about a black man in a hoodie breaking into cars off North Lagoon Drive near the subdivision around Rusty Gans Drive. Two cruisers are dispatched. One driven by Kenny Floyd. The other by Boyd Calhoun. They prowl the area, the mounted spotlights on their patrol cars sweeping the area—until Kenny Floyd sees a suspect matching the description jump over the fence of one of the residents' backyards. He and Boyd both jump out of their cars and give chase, coming up the side of the house and yelling at the man, who runs back into the backyard and beneath a porch. The two officers take up a position at the corner of the house, identify themselves as police officers—something they haven't done until now—and yell for the man to raise his hands and walk toward them. As he does, Kenny yells *gun, gun, gun* and Boyd fires at the man, four rounds out of the six he fires hitting and killing the man. When they approach the suspect they can see that what Kenny thought was a gun was actually an iPhone and who they thought was the suspect was really sixteen-year-old Antwone Wright who was, as he had hundreds of times before, hopping the fence between his house and his grandmother's to eat a snack she had made for him— homemade chocolate chip cookies."

I was familiar with most of what she had said from reading reports on the investigation and now the trial.

Above us, the Spanish moss draped over the thick, reaching oak limbs gently sways in the late April breeze.

"In a rare move the state's attorney's office actually filed charges—but only against Boyd Calhoun so far."

His trial is going on right now.

Across the way a homeless man is lying on one of the park benches, a nest of black garbage bags and kids' cartoon-themed backpacks surrounding him.

"That happened out on the beach over a year ago," she says. "The other case—the one involving Carmen Sykes—happened in town, not far from here, actually, about three weeks ago and is still under investigation. We should hear any day now whether or not criminal charges are going to be filed."

In one sense, Panama City Beach and Panama City seem like the same town—the beach merely an extension of the town—but in another the two cities might as well be worlds apart. Though Panama City has just under forty thousand residents and Panama City Beach only has around twelve thousand, the beach gets some eleven million tourists each year.

"In the second case, Panama City Police received a call that a white male in a prison uniform was waving a gun around and discharging it off Business 98 near the rescue mission. Downtown has a fairly large homeless population and with it a higher than average percentage of mental illness and PTSD. I can't remember if I mentioned it before, but in the Antwone Wright case a caller also said the suspect had a gun. That happens a lot in these cases—citizens calling in give dispatch bad information. So Trevon Fisher, a patrol officer with PCPD, is dispatched to check it out. When he pulls up to the mission, there's a few small groups of mostly men milling about—as there almost always is around there. As he's getting out of his car, two men take off running. They were standing in different groups and take off in different directions. He gets back into his vehicle and drives in the direction of the white man in the white prison uniform carrying a gun. This is all according to him. Not a single witness was there when the other patrol cars arrived and none of them have come forward. And since they're homeless . . . Trevon Fisher drives down Allen Avenue in his vehicle looking for the fleeing suspect. He takes a left on East 7th and then another left on Wilson Avenue when he spots the suspect heading south down Wilson. This puts the suspect and the officer in his vehicle heading back toward the mission. They've simply made the block behind it. When Officer Fisher reaches the mission, he parks his car and gets out of it and gives chase on foot. On that side of the mission there are several oak trees spread around a mostly dirt lot. Fisher claims the suspect, Carmen Sykes, stepped out from behind one and starting firing at him. According to him, he didn't even have his weapon drawn at the time. Says he drew it and returned fire. Carmen Sykes, a Desert Storm veteran with mental issues, was killed. He wasn't wearing an inmate uniform. He was wearing a soiled white chef's outfit from working in the mission's kitchen earlier in the day. And though Trevon Fisher continues to swear that he did have a gun, no weapon was ever found, no rounds ever retrieved."

I nod and think about it, impressed by her ability to recall so many details. She obviously has a great mind and an exceptional memory.

Unlike inside the Place, I can hear the sporadic background sounds of downtown from the park. The splash and bubble of the fountains, tires rolling on asphalt, the hums of vehicle motors, the *clack clack* of palm fronds, the *clang clang clang* of flag poles.

"There are two factors in most cases of police shootings involving unarmed men—race and mental health. Unarmed black men are disproportionately shot by police. As are the mentally ill. In these two cases we have a microcosm of the problem."

Continuing to assess potential threats, I scan the park and the buildings and streets beyond. Two kids on skateboards glide down East Oak toward Luverne. A beer truck behind Corner Pocket is being unloaded. A tour bus pulls down toward the Marina Civic Center.

"It's ironic but by not being extreme, by not clearly being on one side or the other, by not being . . . pigeonholeable . . . I get it from all sides."

"*Pigeonholeable?*"

"If it's not a word it should be," she says. "I'm not anti-cop. I'm not anti-white. I don't always side with one side or the other. I'm not secretly hoping that Boyd Calhoun goes down and Trevon Fisher gets off."

"Every time I hear his name I think of Trayvon Martin," I say.

She nods. "I do too."

In South Florida in February of 2012, Trayvon Martin, a seventeen-year-old African-American kid walking back to his dad's fiancé's home from a convenience store with a pack of Skittles and an Arizona Iced Tea was fatally shot by a zealous and racist neighborhood watch member, George Zimmerman.

"Another child who'll never be anything but," I say, blinking my stinging eyes, thinking of Derek Burrell.

"And for Zimmerman to get away with it . . ." she says. "That's what's so heartbreaking, frustrating, enraging. That's why what we're doing matters so much. And that's why it's so important to make sure we're on the side of justice. Not automatically, thoughtlessly for black or blue, left or right, but justice."

I shake my head and let out a harsh little laugh. "Justice," I say.

"Justice *is* attainable," she says.

"And yet so very rarely attained."

"It's why we keep fighting," she says. "And why so many want to silence us."

12

"I t was one of the oddest darned cases I ever worked," Jeff Ferrel is saying. "You betcha. Never do think I'll get the thing upside right."

He's a mild-mannered, middle-aged cop with the Wisconsin State Police who sounds so white and polite at first I think he's messing with me.

I'm sitting in the hallway not far from Malia's room talking to him on the phone.

"Still have no idea who was behind it or what his motive was. But I'll tell you this—that little lady is gol-darn lucky to be alive."

"Would you mind walking me through it?" I ask.

"Not in the least," he says. "On February seventeenth on a particularly cold and icy night, Ms. Goodman was traveling east on Adams Lake Road in heavy snowfall at approximately oh-one-hundred hours when a black Ford 2015 F-250 struck her vehicle, a 2017 beige Honda Accord rental, on the passenger side, driving it into the lake. The lake is very small—more a pond—and is in a secluded, rural area. In the middle of nowhere really. The truck that was used had been stolen from a farm about two miles up the road and was abandoned less than a mile from the scene of the accident or incident or whatever you want to call it. It had been wiped down, but we found a few partial prints. Guy must not be in the system 'cause we got no matches. Found tons of hairs and fibers like you'd expect, so when we catch him we might be able to match something to him, but . . . we gotta find him first. The farmer and his family were all away for the weekend and have ironclad alibis."

"What are the odd aspects of the case?" I ask.

"Well . . . every case has them, right? And this one doesn't have any more than most. I'm just frustrated by it, truth to tell. I just don't have much in the way of suspects or leads. The fact that it seems like it would have to be random but we don't think it is. The timing it would take to pull it off is just . . . Not many people even knew she'd be on the road at that time of night. Let alone *that* road. She only decided to drive out to stay with an old college friend of hers late that night after she received a threatening phone call on her hotel room phone. And remind me to tell you what was strange about that."

"Do you know who she told she'd be traveling?"

"Some of the people who work with her, the friend she was going to stay with, her aunt, and the organizer of her event the next day. We looked at all of them. Didn't turn up anything. I think she was being followed. But if that's the case how did the perpetrators have time to steal the truck and get it into place? It's a conundrum I'll tell you. And why abandon the truck so soon after using it? Why use it in the first place?"

To make it look like an accident, I think. *Like a hit and run.*

"And then there are the tracks in the snow," he is saying. "I think maybe there were two people involved. Ms. Goodman never saw anyone and took a good bump to the head when she got hit, so probably wouldn't remember even if she had. But there were tracks from where the truck was hidden to the center of the road and back—like the perp left the truck idling and walked out into the middle of the road and back. Our theory is that if there were two people, one was in the road to get Ms. Goodman to slow down while the other drove the truck into her. But if it was one person he must have put something on the road. She remembers slowing for something in the road, but doesn't know what it was. She got hit before she got close enough to it to see what it was. But something caused her to slow down—at least enough for him to be able to fly down the small hill and hit her. Like I say, she struck the side of her head on the driver's side window and received a gol-darn awful concussion. The other reason I think it's likely there were two people is them abandoning the stolen truck so soon. We're talking the middle of nowhere. The weather wouldn't have allowed anyone to walk any distance that night, no, sir. Not at all. So someone had to pick up the driver. I think they had two vehicles."

"Any idea why she didn't stay in Rodney's or Tana's room or have one of them come into hers?"

"They weren't with her that weekend," he says. "From what I understand, Mr. Livingston doesn't normally travel with her, but anyway it was a last-minute thing. Ms. Kay already had plans, and Ms. Goodman was nice enough not to make her cancel. Cripes, it was a perfect storm of events conspiring against her."

Or perfectly orchestrated by someone close to her or someone following her, I think.

"What was strange about the phone call to her room?" I ask.

"Oh, yeah . . . So the call doesn't seem to have come through the front desk," he says, pausing a moment for dramatic effect. "Which means it came from inside the hotel—either another room or the courtesy phone in the lobby."

"Which fits the theory that she was followed from the hotel."

"Well, yeah, I guess so," he says. "But if that's the case, how could he also be stealing a truck and setting up the ambush ten miles away, for cripes' sake?"

13

With Malia safely in her room and Dad on her door, Merrill and I are in the hotel's exercise room working out.

We are running next to each other on treadmills that face a back window with a view of the planted shrubbery of the landscaping and the wooded area beyond.

We're the only two people in the facility.

"Know you familiar with the trolley problem," he says.

His words vibrate as they come out between breaths, and a light sheen of sweat covers the exposed skin of his face, arms, and legs.

"The ethical dilemma one?"

"Yeah."

I nod.

The trolley problem is an ethical and psychological dilemma that presents an interesting thought experiment. There are a number of variations, but in its most basic form, a runaway trolley is racing toward five incapacitated people lying on the tracks. You are standing near a lever that if pulled will redirect the trolley onto another set of tracks and save the five people. The only problem is there is a person on the other set of tracks you would be diverting the trolley to. Are five lives more valuable than one? Do you do nothing and let the trolley kill the five people on the first track or do you pull the lever and divert the trolley and kill the one person in order to save the other five?

"How do you answer it?" he says.

"I don't," I say. "Not without knowing more."

The settings of the treadmills are the same, and our pace and movements are so in sync we could be mirror images of each other.

"Such as?"

"I'd want to know more about the people involved," I say.

"But what if you didn't? What if you couldn't?"

"Well, even if I didn't know anything about them, I could tell a few things just by glancing at them."

"Like?"

"Like if any of them were kids," I say. "I'd be more

likely to flip the switch if there were kids among the five. I'd be more likely not to flip it if the single person on the alternate track was a kid and the five were adults."

"But for the sake of the experiment," he says, "let's say you don't know anything about them and based on their appearance they all look about the same."

"I've thought about it a lot over the years," I say, my breath increasingly labored.

"Figured you had."

"And the truth is . . . it's all hypothetical. Has no actual correlation to what you'd really do when you're put in a split-second life-or-death situation. No way to know until you're actually forced to choose."

"Which unlike most people who think about this, you have."

I shrug and wait a moment before responding, taking in a deep breath as I do. "The split-second life-or-death part. As for the theoretical part, I go back and forth," I say. "At times I feel as though I can't pull the lever, can't just kill an innocent person in cold blood—even to save five. It's the difference in passively letting five die and actively killing one. But at other times I think the fact that life has put me in the position to make the decision means I am responsible for it and must act, must be willing to live with the consequences of my actions, but even then the action I might take and be willing to live with is nonaction. I'm not sure as the scenario is set up I would sacrifice one to save five."

He nods. "The fat man on the bridge change that at all?"

The variation that most often accompanies this original scenario has that same trolley hurtling toward the five people incapacitated on the tracks, but instead of standing next to a lever you are standing next to a fat man on a bridge. If you push the fat man off the bridge, he would stop the trolley and save the five people on the tracks. Do you do nothing and let the five people die? Do you push the fat man off the bridge and save the five people?

"If so," I say, "only to make me even less likely to take action, to murder the one in cold blood to save the five."

He nods.

Before I can ask him what he'd do, he says, "What about the villain on the bridge scenario?"

The other variation asks, what would you do if the fat man on the bridge was evil and was responsible for incapacitating the five people on the track in the first place?

I nod. "That changes everything for me. I would toss a killer off the bridge to save the people he was trying to kill, and it wouldn't matter how many there were—one or five or five hundred."

"That is, in fact, something we've both done before,"

he says. "It's not theoretical. We know what we would do."

"True."

"What if the man on the bridge hadn't just tied up the innocent people on the tracks so the trolley would run over them but had a rifle and was firing at them from the bridge?"

"Would make the decision that much more easy," I say. "Cause me to act that much more quickly."

"And if later you found out that you had been lied to," he says, "deceived by the real killer into thinking the man on the bridge was the killer?"

Now I see where he's been headed all along. He has skillfully set me up in a way only he could. I should have known this wasn't just a random, hypothetical ethical conversation.

I nod and blink back tears. He has created a scenario analogous to the school shooting I had just been involved in, used a well-known ethical dilemma I had thought about many times before against me after causing me to lower my defenses.

"What if instead of you on the bridge next to the innocent fat man with the gun it was me?" he asks. "And what if I was the one who pushed him off only to later find out that he and I had been set up by the real killer? He was shooting at the five people because he believed he was doing what was right in the same way I had thrown him off the bridge to stop the trolley because I thought I was doing what was right. Would you blame me? Would you condemn me? Would you hold me responsible for something I did with the best of intentions? Would you think that I should feel guilty and responsible and ashamed for the rest of my life because of something the real killer did?"

14

The next day when Merrill and Malia arrive at the Bay County Public Library on 11th Street for her signing, protesters are blocking the doors.

As he pulls up to park, he says, "How you want me to handle this? Movin' 'em or makin' a hole through the middle of 'em's not a problem, but I know you have certain ways you want things done."

"I do," she says.

"And since I work for you . . ."

"And therefore are a reflection on me . . ."

"When your safety's not at risk," he says, "I will, ah, comport myself in whatever manner you most prefer."

She smiles. "It's pretty simple and straightforward. Don't assault people."

"Ever?" he asks, his voice rising slightly.

"Pretty much," she says, continuing to smile, enjoying their interaction. "Guard," she adds. "Don't attack."

"Like the dogs?" he says, slipping into his street Ebonics. "I a guard dog, not a attack dog?"

"Well, yeah, I guess. If you like."

"Does I's or does I's not hike my leg?"

"It's not the hiking but what comes after it that concerns me most," she says.

"It's pretty simple and straightforward," he says, mimicking her to near perfection. "The two main motivations for the hike and options once you have are markin' territory and lickin' balls."

"Best to avoid both of those when we're out in public," she says.

"Got it," he says as they step out of the car.

"I knew you would."

When they near the main entrance a few moments later, they can see and hear the protesters.

Ten mostly middle-aged, mostly white, mostly men hold homemade signs aloft, shout out slogans and chants, and form a barricade across the doors.

"Crawl back under your rock and hide. Don't bring your lies inside. You can't take our guns or bullets or knives. What really matters are blue lives. You're not a lady to be quite blunt. You're what rhymes with publicity stunt."

"Guard not attack," Merrill reminds himself.

Beside him, Malia squeezes his shoulder and laughs.

As annoying as the protesters are, it is to a quiet young man across from them that Merrill's attention is drawn to.

So pale as to almost be albino, he has stringy blond hair with bangs that fall down into his nearly invisible eyebrows. His soft, pale blue eyes are locked onto Malia. Standing perfectly still, he stares at her with a blank expression on his face, his passivity spooky.

When they reach the protesters, Malia says, "Excuse me," and tries to pass by.

No one in the group gives any ground, and someone in the back mutters, "There is no excuse for you."

The protesters, who are lined up in two rows to block the two front double doors completely, continue to chant. As they do, they also extend their handheld signs to within inches of her face.

"I have a book signing event inside the library and the freedom and the right to enter the building and conduct it."

She is speaking in a normal tone of voice to people who are yelling and chanting and not listening.

A tall, skinny, elderly librarian with long gray hair is attempting to open the doors from the inside.

None of the doors will open more than an inch or so before being stopped by the heels of the protesters.

The librarian is saying something, and though Merrill is sure it has to do with them moving away from the door, nothing she says can be heard.

She gestures to Malia and says something, then holds up her phone and taps in 9-1-1.

"Why are you all so afraid of what I have to say?" Malia asks.

"You're a liar," one of the men shouts back at her. He's a little man with wavy brown hair and a bushy mustache. "You put police officers' lives in danger."

The conversation they're having is interjected between chants, but part of it is still being cut off.

"That's simply not true," Malia says. "I work hard to support police and make their jobs better and safer. My dad was a cop. So was my husband. And he was killed in the line of duty."

"Bet that made you happy," another man shouts.

Merrill takes a tighter grip on Malia's arm and pulls her back a little farther from the group. He had been expecting her to lunge at the man or at least lash out, but she does neither.

"I was devastated," she says. "He's a big part of the reason I do the work I do."

"Getting other cops killed?"

"Fighting for good police and good policing."

"You sure you don't want me to make a hole?" Merrill asks. "I can get you in there."

"But then no one else can come and go, so what's the use?"

"How do we know you didn't kill him?" one of the other men yells.

"Cop killer!" another one yells.

This time it is Malia who squeezes Merrill's arm, her fingers digging into his skin, but she still manages not to say or do anything reactionary to the small group of provocateurs.

"Your restraint is inspiring," Merrill says. "It's only exceeded by your hand strength."

"Oh, sorry," she says, laughing. "Didn't realize I was . . ."

"All good," Merrill says. "What's the plan exactly?"

"We wait for the cops," she says, "to come and remove these unruly people."

"Then might I suggest we wait over there?" he asks, nodding to a spot under the covered entryway about ten feet away.

She shakes her head. "That might appear like we're backing down or giving up. We're doing neither. We're just not resorting to violence to get inside in order to exercise our constitutional rights."

"I see," he says, nodding. "Good to know what we're doing."

Merrill glances back over to where the young albino-looking boy had been. He's no longer there.

Turning and scanning the entire area, he sees that he is gone.

The group continues to chant hateful slogans and yell obscene accusations and expletive-laced invectives.

"How are you able to maintain such incredible self-control?" Merrill asks.

"Lots of practice."

"But when they say what they do about your husband," he says.

"Some of them say worse about my son," she says. "Those are the ones I have the most difficulty with."

Merrill frowns and nods.

A few moments later when a single patrol car with a lone cop in it pulls up, Merrill can pretty well guess how things are going to go.

As the softish, thirty-something, white PCPD officer walks up, he looks perplexed.

"What's going on here?" he says.

"These people are blocking the doors," Malia says, "refusing to let anyone enter or exit the library."

The cop looks back over at the protesters. "I'm gonna need y'all to move away from the door."

"We have a constitutional right to protest," one of them says.

The others around him agree.

"But not to block traffic," he says. "Let's go."

"We're not going anywhere," another man in the group says.

"Oh, yes you are," the cop says. "One way or another."

Merrill can tell that the cop is in over his head.

"Come on," the cop says. "Move it along."

No one moves.

The cop approaches the group.

"Remember," the little man with wavy hair and mustache says, "just like we went over it."

"If you move on your own and peacefully," the cop says, "you can protest right over there, but if I have to move you, you're done for the day."

"We're not moving."

"Hell yes you are," the cop says, and grabs the closest man by the arm.

As he does, all the members of the group lock arms and ease to the floor, creating a large mass of interlocking deadweight.

"If you don't let me move them it's gonna be a while," Merrill says. "He'll have to wait for enough cops to come and help him cuff and carry all of these morons to a police van."

She shakes her head. "We'll wait."

"It's going to delay your signing and throw off your schedule for the rest of the day, and chances are whoever came for the signing isn't gonna wait around for it anyway."

"But I am," she says. "And I'm going to do it. Even if I'm the only one in there. No way these little fuckers are stopping me from going into that library today. No way."

15

"We're in most places about two weeks on average," Tana is saying. "Eventually people find out where Malia is staying and begin to come by to try to see her or to leave things for her. Not just letters either. Gifts and flowers and candy too. Clothes sometimes. Mixtapes. Homemade arts and crafts. It's crazy how much love she gets. Hate too, I guess."

I nod.

Tana and I are in Malia's room about to go through the recent mail that has arrived. Rodney, who was in here when we started, has been in and out since then.

"We've never watched it particularly closely," she says. "Have no idea who drops off what. Never been especially careful with any of it. I just open and read it. Pass along anything I think Malia needs to see or would like to have."

"Except for the oatmeal cookies," Rodney says. "They're all for me."

I didn't realize he had slipped back into the room.

"Yeah, there are certain things she doesn't want," Tana says. "She's good about letting us take anything we want."

"I might get certain kinds of chocolate too," Rodney adds.

"I take anything with coconut in it," Tana says. "Neither of them care for it."

"So," I say, trying to get her back on track, "Malia receives three types of mail and—"

"Three?" she asks.

"Mail forwarded from the home office in L.A.," I say. "Mail sent to the hotel she's staying in. And mail hand delivered to the hotel."

"Oh, yeah, I guess so."

"And it all comes to the front desk and is placed in a box that you then get and go through?" I say.

"Yeah," she says. "Depending on the hotel size and staff, sometimes they'll have someone run it up to me, but most of the time I pick it up. And sometimes it requires me to get a luggage cart to be able to."

Rodney retrieves some papers off Malia's desk and without another word is gone again.

"And the three vintage postcards with the typed

threats on them were hand delivered?" I ask. "Left at the front desk?"

She nods. "They were inside envelopes. There was no postage on the postcards or the envelopes. In fact, there was nothing on the envelopes at all. No name. No address. No markings of any kind."

"So whoever delivered it would've had to verbally tell the desk clerk who it was for," I say.

She seems to think about it. "Yeah, I guess they would. Unless . . . Sometimes the box is big enough to be visible behind the desk. Almost always has her name on it. It's possible he could've tossed it in the box when the desk clerk was away."

"Were the envelopes sealed?" I asked.

She nods. "They were. I've been thinking about them since you told me about the connections and . . ."

"Yeah?"

"Well, I can't swear to it—like I said we haven't been the most organized with any of it—and I wasn't even aware of the connections until you pointed them out, but . . . I'm fairly sure that while the postcard threats in Madison and Chicago came before the attempt on Malia, the one in Atlanta came afterward."

"Really?"

"Not sure what it means—if anything—but yeah, I'm fairly certain. Didn't stand out or mean anything at the time, but thinking back . . . I don't know. I think so."

"That's very interesting. Thanks for letting me know that. Have you been able to remember if there have been any other vintage postcards from any other towns?"

"Sorry," she says, shaking her head, "but not that I can recall."

"What happens to the mail after it's opened?"

"We box it all up, and before we leave an area, we ship it back to the office," she says. "We keep everything. There's a woman in L.A. who sends Thank You notes to everyone and even writes letters to certain critics—especially when there's been a misunderstanding and we can clarify our position on something. Like most things, I write a lot of those—the main body of the responses anyway—then she sticks in the addresses, salutations, the complimentary close, etc."

"Do you think you could have someone at the office go through the old mail and look for vintage postcards?"

Her wide-eyed, opened-mouthed expression says *yikes*. "There's so much of it. I can ask, but even if she's willing . . . it'll take a while."

"Okay," I say. "It will help if she can."

She makes a note to call the office about searching through the mail. "You ready to go through today's mail?"

I nod.

"How would you like to do it?" she asks. "I thought we could just pour it out on the extra bed and carefully rummage through it."

"That works," I say, handing her a pair of latex gloves, "but put these on first and be very careful with everything."

As she snaps on the gloves, she says, "This should be almost or completely exclusively from the office. Since we've only been here a few days, most people won't even know we're here."

"But what does it say about them if they do," I say.

"True," she says, and gives a little seemingly involuntary shudder.

We dump the contents of the two gray plastic mail crates onto the bed and begin to scatter it around and organize it.

"For now let's just separate it based on the exterior of the packages only," I say. "If you see anything obviously or particularly threatening put it to the side, but I'm most interested in seeing if anything has been mailed to or dropped off at this hotel."

It takes us a while but eventually we find only a single piece of mail that had been hand delivered to the hotel—a plain white sealed envelope with a vintage Greetings from Panama City, Fla. postcard inside. The typed note on the postcard reads, "Florida, where people move to die. Rally all you want, you'll never survive your brief visit to the Redneck Riviera."

16

That night Anna and I go out on a date.

Actually, it's a kind of parallel double date.

Malia and Young Denzel are on a date. I am providing security from a nearby table, and Anna is with me.

"Sorry our date is under these circumstances," I say.

"Hey, I'll take what I can get," she says. "I'm very happy just to be here with you."

We are sitting on the upper back deck of Uncle Ernie's in St. Andrews overlooking the bay as a perfect late April day fades into evening.

To the west, beyond the bay and the tall buildings of Panama City Beach bordering the far side, the setting sun is slowly inching toward the gloaming of the horizon.

Uncle Ernie's is in a late 1800s house built on the edge

of the bay. It had been the home of Uncle Ernie and Jessie Morris in the early 1900s and is one of the oldest buildings in St. Andrews. And though the indoor part is air-conditioned, the back porch has the view and the music.

The advantage of providing security on the upper deck is that there is only one entrance/exit. The disadvantage is there is only one entrance/exit. If someone tries to attack Malia, I will see them coming, but if they get the jump on us, we're trapped.

Malia has a table in the far back corner overlooking the bay. I was set up a few tables away between her and the entrance.

"Young Denzel and Malia sure seem to have hit it off," Anna is saying.

"Yes, they do."

"What's his real name by the way?" she asks.

"Khyree Todd," I say.

"Perhaps we should start calling him that," she says.

I nod.

Though I'm having to look around continuously, scanning the area for potential threats, I spend as much time staring at Anna as possible.

"You are so beautiful," I say.

"Thank you," she says. "I'll never ever get tired of the way you look at me."

From a small stage area on the opposite side of the rooftop dining area, Jace Smith, the regular troubadour here, is performing an acoustic cover of the Statler Brothers' "Flowers on the Wall."

An accomplished musician and singer, and an excellent entertainer, Jace toured the world as part of Rick Springfield's band in the mid-eighties.

"Is it difficult not to order a drink?" Anna asks.

I shake my head.

"How's that going?" she asks.

"Haven't made any real headway toward sobriety or recovery," I say. "Haven't been to a meeting or addressed it in any way other than talking to Dave. But . . . I also haven't had a drink since we started working for Malia."

She nods, but there is nothing in it but non-judgmental acknowledgement of what I've said.

I look around again and we each take another bite of our food.

I'm having the grilled grouper imperial, and she's having the grilled mahi-mahi.

"I did have a couple of drinks just before we started working for her, but none since," I say, "and it hasn't been an issue."

She nods again, again without communicating anything but transmission received.

"I'm not ready to climb up those steps again," I say. "Not ready to go back to AA."

"Okay," she says. "I understand."

"Do you?"

"I think I do," she says. "It's not something you can do until you're ready to anyway, and I so get wanting a break from a program. And as you said . . . it's not an issue at the moment."

"Your understanding makes me want to be sober," I say.

"That's so sweet."

"It's just my reaction to your unconditional love. Let's have a drink to celebrate."

At first, she's not sure if I'm serious, but starts laughing as I do.

After our main courses, Malia and Khyree come over and join us at our table for dessert.

"I love this place," Malia says to me. "Another great choice. And the music . . . he's so good. And so funny."

"He takes requests," Khyree says. "Something you want to hear before we go?"

"Well," Malia says, "we've got to get him to do "Jesse's Girl." I mean come on."

I step over and make the request, which Jace agrees to under one condition—that Anna and Malia sing it with him, which they gladly do.

As they finish, they receive an enthusiastic round of applause from all the patrons and wait staff.

When they return to the table laughing breathlessly, Malia says, "That's the most fun I've had in—all of this, the date and everything—is the most fun I've had in . . . I can't remember the last time I've had this much . . . Who'm I kidding? I can't remember the last time I had fun."

After we've finished our desserts and paid for our meals and tipped Jace for the great entertainment, Malia informs me in front of Khyree that she will be riding back to the hotel with him.

"But you just met him," I say, then turning to him, "It's nothing personal. I like you a lot, but she just met you and—"

"John," Malia says, "I just met you too. I'll be fine. I'm a good judge of character."

"Everybody thinks they're a good judge of character," I say.

"You'll be following us," she says. "Besides, he'll be coming up to my room, so if he wanted to do anything to me . . . that would be the—"

"Oh, I plan to do things to you," Khyree says.

"But—" I begin.

"John," Malia says again, "I wasn't asking. I was informing."

17

"I love hotel room sex," Anna is saying.

Our naked bodies are still entwined on the firm bed in the dim, cold room.

"Me too," I say. "I mean, I love sex with you anywhere, but hotel sex is amazing."

While Malia and Young Denzel are in her room doing whatever they are doing—probably something not unlike what Anna and I had just done—Merrill is in the chair at the end of the hallway sitting sentinel.

Since Taylor is spending the night with my dad and his wife Verna and Johanna is at her mom's, Anna gets to stay for an extended visit. She plans to leave when I go out in the hallway for the overnight shift, and Merrill comes in here to sleep.

"Can we do it again?" she asks.

"Absolutely," I say.

"Do we have time?"

"We do," I say. "And I'm going to need it. Give me just a few minutes and . . . we'll commence with round two."

"God, I'm so much happier when I'm with you," she says.

She leans down and takes hold of the closest corner of the mass of covers at the bottom of the bed and draws them up onto us.

"I am too," I say.

And in that moment of both happiness and the expression of that happiness, I am struck with an overwhelming and oppressive sense of guilt.

Unbidden and unexpected in this ecstatic and serene moment, images of Derek Burrell dying fill my mind.

Me running up. Him turning, aiming his gun. Me raising my weapon. Aiming. Firing. The return blast of his shotgun. Deafening. The high-pitched hum following. Him falling. His parents appearing on the floor beside him. His mother yelling, *You killed him. Why? Why did you kill my kid?*

A voice inside my head saying, *How can you let yourself be happy after what you've done? What kind of man can do that to a kid and then go on like nothing happened?*

"I'm sorry," I say to Anna, "but I may have to take a rain check on a return engagement."

"What is it?" she asks. "Are you okay?"

18

"I don't think it was a serial," Detective Blake Greeley is saying. "Don't think it was random neither. That man was in that room to get that woman. Not sure rape was part of his plan either. Could've been. No way to know for sure, but I think he was there to slice her up."

Blake Greeley is a detective with the Chicago Police Department.

It's early the next morning, and I'm speaking to him by phone in the hallway a few minutes before Merrill relieves me and I get a couple hours of sleep before the day's activities.

"What makes you say that?" I ask.

"You gonna rape a woman and you have a weapon," he says, "whatta you use the weapon for?"

"To control her," I say. "Subdue her if you have to."

"Exactly," Greeley says. "You say, Hey, see this big fuckin' knife? Be still and let me stick my dick in you, or I'll cut you with it. Scream or fight me or try to get away and I'll cut you with it. He didn't do any of that. Just started attacking her. No warning. No threat. Just an attack. A vicious one at that."

I think about that. The guy could've been a frenzied rapist killer or a killer who rapes post mortem, but in general Greeley's right. The modus operandi isn't usual.

"And another thing," he says, "the guy's a fuckin' acrobat. Breaks into her third-floor room through her balcony. Your average rapist ain't gonna do that, am I right? If he's gonna break in at all, it's probably gonna be a dwelling or maybe an apartment, but whatever it is it's gonna be on the first fuckin' floor. He's not gonna Dick Grayson some shit into some random room he had no idea who's inside of."

He's right.

"Nah, he was there for that lady in particular," he says. "He knew which room was hers. And he was there for her. Cut her up. Kill her. Violently rape her. I don't know, but whatever it was, it was for her."

"You have any leads on who it might have been?" I ask.

"I gotta guy I'm looking at," he says. "Don't have much on him but I like him for it. He's one of these white nationalist survivalist dudes. He's protested some of her rallies. He's sent her some hate mail. He's a loner—not part of any group. Physically, he could do it. He's young and strong and agile. I'm watching him. Closely. If he leaves town or anything I'll give you a heads-up, but that's all I can do. I can't give out a suspect's name or anything. 'Specially since I'm the only one who thinks he's a suspect."

"Understood. Her assistant said he left behind a big hunting knife."

"Biggest bastard I ever seen," he says. "We lifted a partial from it, but no match. Must not be in the system."

"Has the guy you like for it been in the system?"

"Nope. He ain't. But get this . . . the partial we have . . it matches a partial a state cop in Wisconsin sent me that he lifted from a truck used in a hit and run on the same lady."

"So the same guy attacked her in both places," I say. "That's helpful to know."

"Not until we find the guy, it ain't," he says. "As far as anything else, we got too much, you know what I mean? I mean, it's a hotel for Chrissakes, so we got more than a few prints, but none we can match to anybody in particular. All kinds of hairs and fibers too. Forensic nightmare."

He pauses, and I wait.

"Tell you one thing for sure," he says. "Guy's good with locks. He was able to pop this one no problem. Good with locks and a fuckin' climber."

"Does that fit with your suspect?"

"I think so, but not everybody here is as convinced. I gotta be honest with you. Some of the other guys like this Aryan Brotherhood banger—supposedly even bragged about it inside after he was popped for somethin' else, but . . . you know how jailhouse snitches are. I don't know, I just get the sense that this is a quiet boy obsessed with this lady in particular, not some gangbanger doin' it for the hell of it, gonna brag about it afterward."

"From what I know of it, I'm with you," I say.

"Another thing about my guy that fits . . . He's maybe a little on the timid or weak side—mentally, I mean. Not takin' nothin' away from the lady, because she deserves all due—she put up one hell of a fight—but he's got a knife and the jump on her, and he still can't close the deal. Makes me think he's new at this. Hell, maybe she's his first. Hell, if he's got it bad enough for her, maybe she's his one and only."

19

"It's not just that American police shoot and kill far more people each year than their counterparts in other developed countries," Malia is saying, "it's that there is a huge racial disparity in who gets shot and how police officers in the United States use force."

We are at Gulf Coast State College where Malia has been invited by Black Students Against Violence to give a speech.

We are in the upstairs conference room of Student Union East where a large crowd of students, faculty, and community members are listening intently—some in agreement, others in anger.

Because the crowd is much larger than expected, a last-minute move of venue has us scrambling to offer her adequate protection.

"Crowd this size," Merrill whispers, shaking his head, "room this open . . . Guy tries something here, be hard as hell to stop him."

I nod.

My dad and brother are here to help, as is a nephew of Merrill's, but we're still not adequately staffed. We also enlisted the help of Khyree Todd, who is more than enthusiastic to look heroic and make a good impression on Malia.

Dad and Jake are positioned up on either side of the stage. Merrill's nephew and Khyree are at the entrances on either side of the room. Merrill and I are moving around the room.

"Police in this country kill black people at disproportionate rates," Malia is saying. "We make up 31 percent of those killed by police but only 13 percent of the population. This disparity is even greater among unarmed suspects. Combined together, racial minorities make up about 62.7 percent of unarmed people killed by police but only account for 37.4 percent of the general population."

Though Malia is speaking without notes or a teleprompter, Tana, who is standing in the back, is mouthing nearly every word along with her.

I step over to her.

"Heard this speech before?" I ask with a smile.

She laughs. "I wrote it."

"I've never seen her use notes or a teleprompter," I say.

"She doesn't," she says. "She memorizes all her speeches."

"Really?" I ask. "Why's that?"

"Remember what I told you about her dyslexia? It's pretty severe. She memorizes everything. Her disability makes what she's accomplished all the more impressive. I keep telling her that this weakness makes her other superpowers all the more astounding, but she's embarrassed about it. You haven't mentioned it to anyone, have you? Please don't."

"I won't. But you're right. It does make all she's accomplished far more impressive."

"And before you go to thinking that this is because of socioeconomic factors such as poverty and unemployment and the like," Malia is saying, "even with those factored in there's still a huge disparity. Black people are far more likely to be arrested for drug-related offenses, but they are not more likely to use or sell drugs. And they make up a disproportionate percentage of the prison population. Are there higher crime rates in certain minority communities? Of course—for the factors I've already mentioned, meaning it's largely an economic, not a racial issue—but studies show that only accounts for about 60 percent of our overrepresentation in prison. That means some 40 percent of the racial disparity of imprisonment rates is attributable to racial bias. Think about this—studies show there is no relationship, no relationship at all, between crime rates in a community and the racial bias observed in police shootings. We can't say that racial bias observed in police shootings is not explainable as a response to local-level crime rates."

I can't tell whether she's aware of it or not but Malia is beginning to lose some of her audience. I can see some of the movement and noises that indicate restlessness and wandering attentions.

"I'm the daughter of a cop. I'm the widow of a cop. I love and appreciate cops. Cops aren't the enemy. Cops are us—people just like us. The problem we're confronting is not the police. It's the lack of vetting and lack of training of those police. Fine upstanding officers, good cops, are calling for reform just as much as we are. They're aware of the racial bias present in the population and how it is reflected in policing practices and mindsets. They know that cops are quicker to shoot black suspects in video simulations. They know that shows up in the field. They know that makes their job more difficult and dangerous. Are there some bad apples in the barrel? Of course. Do they need to be removed? Absolutely. That's why we need better vetting, more strenuous psychological standards, but we also need much, much better training and much more of it. How can you address the problem of racial bias when you're not even aware you have it?"

She pauses for a moment, seems to study her audience.

"At this time I'm going to open it up for questions and comments," she says.

Tana looks at me. "There's a lot more left of her speech. She must sense she's not engaging with them like she'd like to."

Merrill steps over to me and points out a pale young man sitting toward the back of the room, staring at Malia with incredible intensity.

"That's the one I was telling you about from the library," he says. "Creepy little fucker."

"Let's tell the others and all keep an eye on him," I say. "And try to talk to him if we can."

"It's real simple," Malia is saying. "You can ask me anything, you can make any comment you like, but you have to be civil, courteous, and respectful. One brief question or comment stated civilly. We need discourse. We need to be able to disagree agreeably. I don't mind you thinking I'm wrong or telling me. I invite it. I just insist that you do it respectfully. And if you're not respectful you'll be ushered out."

I wonder who she thinks is going to do that. Merrill and I can't be in here guarding her and outside removing disruptive audience members at the same time.

An older white man with a sour expression on a

deeply wrinkled face slowly pushes himself up on his forearm crutches.

"Jerry Edwards from the *Jerry Edwards Show*," he says.

"That's him," Tana whispers to me.

"Who?"

"The ex-cop with the rightwing talk show from Chicago who's so critical of Malia and is always showing up at her events."

"You didn't tell me he was from Chicago," I say.

"Why does that— Oh. That's where she was attacked in her hotel room. I didn't put that together. But he couldn't have done that. He's too crippled to do all that climbing and breaking in and fighting with her."

Because we were talking I missed what Edwards said.

"You know as well as I do that it's voluntary for police agencies to report to the feds about use of force, deadly or otherwise, and without the exact numbers there can't be exact knowledge, and without exact knowledge, there can't be accountability. That's the issue. Accountability. Well, one of the issues. Another is that police can use force just if they feel threatened. That's a very low bar and can lead to abuse. Another key component is how rarely cops are prosecuted for killing unarmed citizens and how few of those are ever found guilty and how few of those ever serve any real time."

"So you're for locking cops up, that it?" Edwards says.

"No, I'm for locking criminals up—no matter what

their profession is. Drug dealer. Cop. Priest. Politician. Movie star. Fringe talk show host."

When Edwards starts to say something else, Malia holds up her hand. "We said one comment or question. You've already had several."

"*We* didn't say that," he says. "*You* did. And rather than trying to silence me, why not agree right here in front of everyone to debate me. I've been asking you for years. What're you so afraid of?"

"Fine."

Tana leans over to me again. "He's so fringe and has such a small audience, she knows he's just trying to use her to raise his profile and increase his following."

"You all heard her," he is saying. "She agreed to debate me. Can't back out now."

A blocky, middle-aged white woman with gray hair and a harsh expression on her face stands on the opposite side of the room from Edwards, and the mic is taken to her. "If you truly support cops the way you say you do, why are you waging a war against them?"

"I'm—" Malia begins, but the woman isn't finished.

"What would your dad and husband say about what you're doing?"

"There is no war on cops," Malia says. "That's an absurd notion. It's a factually unsupported talking point by unethical and irresponsible TV and radio personalities used to whip up a fearful frenzy among their racist and gullible audiences. Facts matter. Truth matters. Or at least it should. The fact is, the truth is, killings of police officers on duty are at near record lows. Partisan political disseminators of misinformation have blamed the Black Lives Matter movement for what they called a wave of violence against the police, but there was no such thing. It's about as safe to be a cop now as it has ever been."

"You could say the same about being a black man in America," the woman says.

Malia nods. "Yes, you could. And, sadly, you'd be right."

The woman opens her mouth but finds she has nothing to say.

20

F ollowing the conclusion of the program, roughly thirty people rush the stage—some with books they want signed, others wanting a picture, most with more to say.

The pale young man from the library event isn't among them, and doesn't appear to be in the room any longer.

Sensing the program was winding down, Merrill and I had made our way toward the stage so we could get on either side of Malia the moment she was finished.

"Malia. Malia. Malia."

As if a pool of reporters trying to ask a question of a reluctant interviewee, many among the thirty are constantly calling her name.

Beyond the aggressive group at the foot of the stage,

most of the three hundred or so in attendance have yet to leave. Instead, they mill around talking and watching.

Suddenly Tana seems to materialize on the stage.

"We're very sorry," she says into the mic, "but Ms. Goodman has to leave immediately in order to make her next appointment—an interview you can hear live on WKGC in just a few minutes. Please tune in for that. Should be a great interview. And join us for a book signing tomorrow at the Books-A-Million on 23rd Street across from the Panama City Mall. Thank you again for coming and have a good evening."

With Dad and Jake leading the way and Merrill's nephew and Young Denzel in the rear, Merrill and I are on each side of Malia as we walk out of the Student Union and across the small campus to the college radio station.

We strongly suggested that she let us put her in the vehicle and drive the short distance, but Malia insisted on walking, saying the stroll in the fresh air was worth the risk.

As we make our way east along the sidewalk, past the Social Sciences building, Malia and Khyree ease toward and fall in step with each other.

When we reach the radio station, Tana and Rodney, who have driven over, are waiting for us outside the building.

While we are determining who will be where during

the interview—it's decided that Merrill and I will be inside the station with Malia, Tana, and Rodney, while the others stand guard outside—Jerry Edwards climbs out of his truck in the handicap parking spot and begins to make his way over toward us.

"You promised me a debate," he yells, still a distance away.

He is moving slowly and steadily on his crutches, stumbling and almost tripping several times as he tries to move far faster than he should.

"Everyone heard you," he is saying. "Can't back out of it this time."

"Haven't backed out of it any other time," she says, more to our group than him.

"Let's get inside," Merrill says. "Don't like standing out here like this."

Malia nods, then to Rodney says, "Deal with him," nodding toward Edwards. "Set up a simple debate soon. Let's get it over with. And I don't want a circus. Just a fair forum with a competent moderator."

"But I was planning to be inside the station with you," Rodney says.

"Why?" she says. "Nothing for you to do in there."

"It's hot out here," Rodney says.

The entire group glances at him in disdainful disbelief.

"Malia," Edwards says as he hears us, "I demand to speak to you now. Right now."

"I've got somewhere I've got to be, Jerry," she says, "but I've instructed Rodney here to set up a debate between us. How long will you be in town?"

"Least as long as you are," he says.

"Oh joy. Well, anyway, we'll do it sooner rather than later. Okay? Happy?"

"I—" he begins.

"Talk to Rodney," she says as we are buzzed into the building.

Though we had searched the building before the presentation at the Student Union, once we have Malia tucked away in the interview studio, we do another complete search of the building, knowing Dad, Jake, and the others are doing the same thing outside.

Taking turns, alternating between standing outside the studio watching Malia through the glass window and sweeping the station, we carefully but quickly search the other studios, the bathrooms, the small kitchen, the offices and conference room, the closets, the equipment room, and every and all other searchable spaces in the small building.

As we do, we can hear the radio broadcast, which is playing throughout the building on high-end monitor speakers.

"The police are not the problem," Malia is saying.

"And whatever problems there are . . . the police are the solution."

"What do you mean?" the interviewer asks. "Because I know a lot in the community would disagree with you about that."

He is an African-American student named Keith interning at the station.

"Not only is it wrong to say that the police are the problem, but it's simply too broad. It'd be like saying Americans are the problem. Sure, those causing the problems are Americans, but not all Americans are causing the problems. But it's not just that it's too broad. It's just not true. The police aren't the problem. The training, or lack thereof, and policing techniques and procedures—they are the real problems."

"But isn't that semantics?" Keith asks. "Aren't police training, or lack thereof, and policing techniques and police procedures and bad police the police?"

"What's the definition of racism?" Malia asks.

"Ah . . ."

"Isn't it judging an entire group of people based on the character or actions of one member of that group or a small sampling of that group? If a black man robs or rapes you and you judge all black men to be robbers or rapists, that's a simple definition of racism, right? Well, if you judge all police to be bad because of a very, very few bad police, wouldn't that be policeism?"

Keith chuckles a little but doesn't seem to know how to respond.

After an awkward moment passes, he says, "Okay . . . Well, you're certainly one of the most outspoken supporters and critics of the police. Let's get back to something you've criticized the police for in the past. Something you call the 'militarization of the American police department.'"

"It's true," Malia says. "The federal government has helped the militarization of police in unprecedented ways in this country. Police departments around the states have obtained military-grade equipment at little to no cost through federal programs. They have then on many occasions deployed equipment designed for war-type situations—such as tear gas, rubber bullets, sound cannons, mine-resistant armored trucks, and other armed forces special weapons—often against peaceful protesters. These programs have transferred surplus military-grade equipment from the Pentagon to the local police department without requiring any training or oversight. And it gets worse. This equipment comes with a terrible set of strings attached. The departments receiving it have to use it at least once a year to keep it. Think about that. Use it or lose it. The Obama administration banned some of this equipment, but it didn't go far enough, and there's a loophole. These departments can bypass the federal program and regulations entirely by purchasing the equipment themselves."

"It's absolutely frightening," Keith says. "Like martial law or the military policing civilians. Well, I could keep asking you questions all night, but we have callers on the line waiting patiently to talk to you, so I'll just ask one more before we go to the phone lines. What is the solution? How can we fix the problem of the police?"

"Again, I don't see the police as the problem," she says. "Don't see them as a problem in need of fixing, but . . . there are steps we can take to make sure that we get the best police forces everywhere, not just in some cities."

"What are those?"

"We must have more rigorous recruiting, interviewing, testing, hiring practices," she says. "We've got to weed out the bad seeds before they ever begin to grow in our departments. Then we have to have more and better training—training that deals with all the issues facing law enforcement, including racial biases and how to deal effectively and compassionately with the mentally ill. And we've got to have accountability. Every officer and every vehicle should have a camera—cameras that can't be turned off or muted. And we must have community involvement and oversight. Community policing programs and civilian oversight committees are among the most effective ways to get the police departments we deserve."

"Okay, you're listening to *Community Talk Time*. I'm Keith Greene, and I'm joined this evening by author and activist Malia Goodman. And now to a few questions from listeners."

"Malia," an older white female voice says with overfamiliarity, "how would you respond to your critics that say that all you're trying to do is sell books?"

"I'd say they're right, except for the 'all' part," Malia says. "I think everyone should buy and read my books, but the work I do isn't just to sell books. There are far easier, safer, and more effective ways to do that."

"Next caller," Keith says.

"How can you be so supportive of the bastards who killed your only son?" an angry white male voice asks. "What the hell kind of mother are you? I mean for fu—"

"Next caller," Keith says.

"When you leave Panama City," a man says in a gravelly whisper, "it'll be in a body bag. Community police that, bitch."

21

"I'm not sure I'm an alcoholic," I say.

Dave's eyebrows shoot up, and he gives me an interested though skeptical look.

"I know how it sounds," I say. "I know how dangerous it is even to think. But . . ."

Dave Lloyd and I are sitting on the side patio of Millie's following one of his gigs.

Millie's is a restaurant inside the first floor east corner of the old Sherman Arcade building in Downtown Panama City. One of the oldest and coolest buildings in the old downtown district, the Sherman Arcade has an open breezeway down its center—with businesses off either side on the ground level and apartments on the second floor.

I had arrived in time to hear the last couple of songs

Dave played, which included "Into the Mystic," 'Ain't No Sunshine," and, by request from me, Sting's "Fragile."

Downtown is mostly dead.

The tables of the courtyard where we sit are now empty.

Inside Millie's the staff is cleaning up and prepping for tomorrow's lunch. A few people are still drinking and shooting pool inside Corner Pocket next door. But neither group is visible to us.

The occasional passerby passes by on the sidewalk, the occasional car rolls by on Harrison, but these occur so infrequently Dave and I can go for long stretches with the sense that we're the only two people in the abandoned downtown district.

"It has been a part of my identity for so long," I say, "but now I'm just not so certain it should be. I'd just like to explore the possibility with you."

He nods. "Of course."

It's a testament to Dave's compassionate nature and his skill as a counselor that I feel like I can talk to him about something as radical and controversial as this.

Over the past several days we have frequently spoken by phone and texted continuously, and he already feels more like a trusted friend than a professional counselor.

"I know the idea is anathema," I say, "and I know that every active alcoholic in denial has believed they aren't one, but . . . I'm not in denial, and I'm not saying that I'm not an alcoholic—just that I might not be. And I'm coming at it from the other end—from decades of thinking I was one. It may all just come down to semantics, but it might not."

"I understand," he says.

"Part of the reason I want to share it with you is so I can hear it out loud when I say it, and so you can question anything I say and hold me accountable. I don't feel like I'm rationalizing or justifying, but I want to know what you think."

He nods. "I'll give you my feedback," he says, "but alcoholism is a self-diagnosed disease. You have to determine for yourself if you're an alcoholic or not because that's the point where recovery begins. Family, friends, and coworkers can tell us they think we are, but we have to get to the point where we can admit we are powerless over alcohol and that our lives have become unmanageable."

"I've worked the steps many times," I say. "And I've taken many of the self-tests over the years— Do you crave alcohol? Have you lost control? Do you drink alone or in secret? Have you lost interest in other activities and hobbies that used to bring pleasure? Is drinking a compulsion? Have you had legal problems or problems with relationships, employment, finances?"

"Don't forget that a high-functioning alcoholic might be able to answer no to all or most of those."

A high-functioning alcoholic is able usually with the help of an enabler, to maintain respectable, even high-profile lives. They often have a nice home, a mostly functioning family, good job, and a few friends. But they also have a secret—a hidden addiction to alcohol.

"My mom was an alcoholic," I say. "She had the disease. She never really seriously sought treatment. She died from it."

"I'm very sorry to hear that," he says.

"I feel like I know what alcoholism looks like," I say. "And I know how serious and dangerous and deadly a disease it is. I'm not making light of it in any way."

"I'm sure you do," he says, "but . . . just remember it can look like a lot of different things. There's no one way to be an alcoholic."

"Absolutely," I say. "I've been around and worked with a lot of alcoholics over the years—in AA, as a minister, as a chaplain. And I know I have certain traits or characteristics of an alcoholic."

"It's probably a spectrum like so many things," he says.

I nod. "And it may just come down to that—that what I'm really saying is that . . . I think I might not be where I thought I was on the spectrum. It seems like more than that, but maybe that's it."

He continues to nod.

"The thing is . . ." I say, ". . . I think my mom's alcoholism caused me to both fetishize alcohol and alcoholism and to identify with and interpret my own relationship with that fetish in certain ways. Something I think led to an unhealthy dichotomy, a dangerous all-or-nothing mentality. If alcoholism is a symptom of a deeper, darker unhealthy way of thinking . . . then maybe changing the paradigm through which I've viewed and interpreted all of this for so long is what is most needed."

"Interesting," he says.

And he really does seem to be interested on a variety of levels.

"I'm questioning whether I have an actual chemical dependency on alcohol," I say, "or if it's purely psychological."

"Does it matter?" he asks. "Doesn't it come down to the same thing?"

"Maybe," I say. "But . . . the thing is . . . because of my mom's addiction and my relationship to alcohol, I've always ascribed to it this nearly mythological power, and I think that has been the biggest component of my so-called addiction. And I realize how risky it is to call it my so-called addiction, but . . . I think it's possible that if I address the fetishistic aspect of alcohol and alcoholism, I might be able to strip it of its power over me. Of course, this could all be total bullshit, which is why I'm saying it out loud and asking for your feedback."

He nods.

"But the thing is . . . following the death of Derek Burrell, everything changed. I was still drinking, but it didn't mean as much, didn't have the power it once did. I found myself not givin' much of a fuck about anything, including alcohol, and suddenly, when it was drained of its power, it didn't have a hold on me, and that's when I began wondering about all this."

"That is very interesting," he says. "I think the biggest question is if it's temporary or not. Is it because of the circumstances, because you're still in shock and depressed and . . . or is it that this experience has led you to new insight and more truthful experience?"

"I'm not drinking much at all right now, but for the first time in my life, I'm not drinking because I'm trying not to drink. I'm not scared to have a drink. And I have been able, and that's it. It's like for the first time I'm not *drinking* or *not drinking*, I'm just living, and alcohol isn't an issue."

"What you're saying is risky and radical and dangerous," he says, "and it would be far safer to get back in AA and work the steps and—"

"What if I work the steps like this?" I ask. "While drinking occasionally."

"There's nothing to say you can't," he says. "Some non-alcoholics work the steps as a program for spiritual growth, but . . . I don't know."

"I'm working this case right now," I say, "and in the

past when I was drinking I'd sometimes become so obsessed with a case that I'd stop drinking, but this isn't like that. It's unlike anything I've experienced before. It's hard to explain."

"I think it's all worth exploring," he says. "It's a good sign that you're willing to submit it to scrutiny."

"I'll go with your and Anna's assessment," I say, "but regardless of how I identify myself or whether I'm in AA or drink or not, it'd be nice if alcohol had no power over me."

DRIVING BACK TOWARD THE HOTEL, I call Anna.

"Sorry to wake you," I say.

"No, I'm glad you called," she says, her voice soft and sleepy.

"I just met with Dave again, and I wanted to share something with you."

"Okay."

I tell her what I told Dave.

She listens and gives me enough verbal responses that I feel heard and understood.

"Whatta you think?" I ask. "Does it scare you?"

"I told you," she says. "Nothing scares me where you're concerned. And what you're sayin' makes a certain kind of sense. It really does. If you can get to the place where alcohol has no power over you, then—"

"I'm at that place now," I say. "The question is—can I stay here?"

"I sure hope you can," she says.

"You know when I knew I was in this place?" I say. "When I felt my freest and alcohol had no more power over me?"

"When?"

"When you responded the way you did about my drinking," I say. "You took the power out of it for me by what you said."

"Which thing?" she asks. "I say so much."

"That you loved me and weren't going anywhere whether I drank or not."

"It's true."

"The things you said about the kind of man I am even when I'm drinking," I add. "That kind of unconditional love and acceptance and your support clarified something inside me, helped me in ways I can't even explain. Thank you. Thank you so much for that and everything you are."

22

I'm reading a new book about prison chaplaincy while in the hotel hallway watching Malia's door when Tana slowly opens hers and looks out.

"Everything okay?" I ask.

"Had a bad dream, I guess."

I close the book, place it on the floor beside my chair, and stand up.

I'm on administrative leave from my part-time prison chaplaincy position right now too. The timeframe for my leave from it runs roughly the same as that of my sheriff's investigator's job. The time away has done me good, and I look forward to getting back to it. Sometimes I think I should just leave chaplaincy altogether, but something inside me won't let me. Tonight I've been wondering if it's because, like alcoholism, it's part of my identity and has been for so long.

"Everything's okay," I say. "All quiet out here. You're safe."

"Thank you," she says.

"Want me to check your room for you?" I ask. "I can do a quick sweep of it while you stand in the doorway if it would make you feel better."

"Mind if I just sit out here and talk to you for a few?"

"Not at all."

While she steps back inside to get her keycard, I grab a chair for her and place it next to mine.

"You okay?" I ask when we are seated next to each other.

She shrugs. "Not sure what I should do," she says. "It's . . . The prospect of going out on my own is scary, and Malia is begging me to stay. I just . . . don't want to make a big mistake."

I nod. "It's rarely easy to know what to do. So many unknowns and variables. But very few things are irreversible, and any time we feel like we've stepped off the path we're meant to be on we can usually just take a few steps and get back on it."

"You think so?"

"And when it comes to opportunities for growth, for new challenges and experiences, we tend to regret the ones we don't take."

She nods. "That's probably true. But what if staying is an opportunity too? Rodney keeps saying I'm going to have more and more opportunities. Of course, Malia has been saying that for a while now, and they mostly haven't materialized."

"With most decisions like this there's no right or wrong choice," I say. "I think sometimes we put way too much pressure on ourselves, believing that we only get one chance to make the correct decision, but I don't think that's too often the case."

"I keep thinking . . . What if I leave and something happens to Malia? What if I could've stopped it if I had stayed? But then I think, what if I stay and something happens to me? Or what if something happens to Malia and I could've taken up her mantle, stepped in and continued the work, kept the momentum going? Of course, that can't happen until she lists me as a co-writer and lets me start speaking some, being out front more. And I'm not sure she's ever going to. Sometimes it seems like it but then others it seems like she never will."

I nod but don't say anything.

She seems to slip into deeper thought about it all, and I don't interrupt her.

When she resurfaces a few moments later, she says, "You any closer to finding out who's behind the attacks on Malia?"

"Some, maybe," I say.

"I don't want to call anybody out . . ." she says.

"But?"

"But . . . Rodney's been acting strange for a while now, and it's getting worse. I don't know . . . he just . . . He disappears for long stretches of time. He's not where he's supposed to be a lot of the time. He's just acting . . . so strange."

"You think he has something to do with the threats or attacks on Malia?"

"What? No. Nothing like that. That never even crossed my— He adores Malia. He's her biggest— No. Never. Nothing like that. I just was concerned that he might not be able to look out for her like he should if I leave. I was hoping you might find out what's going on with him and keep an even closer eye on Malia if I decided to leave."

Maybe that's what she meant, but I find it doubtful. Whether intentional or subconscious her comments and questions about Rodney come right after she asked if I was getting anywhere with finding out who was threatening and attacking Malia.

As I start to say something to her, her eyes grow wide, and her face fills with fear as she looks over my shoulder.

I spin around and come up out of my seat, reaching instinctively for my weapon.

Coming through the stairwell door are four men in all black SWAT-type outfits, including riot helmets, face shields, gas masks, Kevlar tactical body armor, black military boots, and each carrying 12-gauge black pump shotguns—all pointed at us.

23

Realizing I can't get to my weapon, I try to tap my phone in my front left pocket, hoping it might call Merrill since he was the last person I spoke to. I then raise my hands.

Beside me, Tana does the same.

I can tell from her breathing that she is starting to panic.

"Just breathe," I say to her. "Long, slow, deep breaths. Let them out slowly. Just concentrate on your breathing. Nothing else."

Though the four men look to be part of an elite tactical law enforcement unit or response team, there are no badges or patches or insignia or identification of any kind on their uniforms.

Using hand signals to communicate, they are quiet

and efficient, appearing to be an experienced and well-trained unit.

Fanning out around us, they continually communicate with each other and glance down the hallway.

One of them—the one standing closest to me—says something, but I can't make it out because of his gas mask.

When I indicate that I can't hear him, he looks to the other men for confirmation, which they give.

Shaking his head, he lowers his shotgun, holding it with one hand now.

Pulling his gas mask down slightly he says, "Which room is Malia Goodman's?"

I shake my head.

"You don't know, or you won't say?" he asks.

One of the other men says something that might have been, "Of course he knows. He's here protecting her."

"And doing a damn fine job of it too," the guy in front of me says.

"Who are you?" I ask. "Why are you here?"

I can guess the answers to both questions. I only ask them to stall—though I don't know why. There are four of them. They all have helmets and vests and shotguns. I have no play. I am only prolonging the inevitable.

And the inevitable will be what they do when I refuse to give them Malia.

"We're just here to have a little talk with the—with Ms. Goodman. That's all."

"This is how you come to talk to someone?" I ask. "I'd hate to see how you roll up on someone you have bad intentions toward."

"It's overkill, I know," he says. "But we have to be careful and remain anonymous. I swear all we want to do is talk."

"Oh good," I say. "That's such a relief."

"I mean it," he says. "It's the truth."

"In a lot of ways I'm a professional talker," I say. "As a counselor and teacher and interviewer. And it just so happens that I've got some time on my hands right now."

"Has to be Malia," he says. "And I'm running out of patience. Which room is hers?"

I shake my head. "You have to know I'm not going to tell you," I say.

The man behind Tana jacks a round into the chamber of his shotgun and presses the barrel to the back of her head.

"How 'bout now?" the man in front of me asks.

Tana begins to shake as her breathing becomes more erratic and tears stream down her cheeks.

"We don't want to, but we will splatter her brains all over this hallway if you don't get Malia to open her door," he says. "It's real simple. We have a quick little chat with Malia, or this woman dies and then you, and then we still break down her door and talk to her. 'Course then we'll have to kill her too."

"John, please," Tana says. "Let them just talk to her."

"I can't," I say.

"She would want you too," she says. "She would never ever want you to let them hurt me."

"On three," the man says. "Pull the trigger on three."

Tana becomes hysterical. The man with the shotgun to her head is having to hold her with his other arm now.

I make eye contact with her and try to reassure her, but I'm not sure what's actually communicated.

"One."

He pauses a moment.

Tana's knees buckle, and she grows even more distraught.

As she collapses to the floor, the man holding the gun to her readjusts. Now, she is flat on the floor with his boot on her chest and the barrel of the shotgun pressed against her forehead.

"Two."

I can see the man's trigger finger move into position and twitch a little.

"Thr—"

"Okay," I say. "Okay. Don't shoot. I'll get Malia to open her door. You swear you're just going to talk to her?"

"Swear."

"Okay," I say. "Help her up and let her sit in one of the chairs over there while I get Malia to open up."

As two of the men begin to help Tana into a seat, the others follow me as I move over to my and Merrill's door.

Setting up on either side of the door so they can't be seen from the peephole, they wait as I knock on the door and say, "Malia. Malia, wake up. There's someone here who needs to talk to you."

"Don't tell her that," he says. "Tell her you need to talk to her."

"Oh," I say. "Okay. Malia, it's an emergency. I need to talk to you. Wake up. Come out here. I need your help. Malia."

As the door begins to be unlocked and opened, the two men shove me aside and ram the door.

24

As the two men lower their shoulders to hit the door, their weapons come down.

Just as they're about to hit the door, it opens quickly.

Suddenly without the door there, the two men stumble and lurch forward.

I wrap my arm around the throat of the one on the left and snatch him back into the hallway, as the one on the right stumbles into the dark room.

Slinging the man to the ground, I step on his shotgun and, withdrawing my weapon, press it against his face shield.

He takes his hand off the shotgun and doesn't try to resist.

While one stays with Tana, the other comes up

behind me and presses the shotgun to the back of my head.

"Let him up," he says to me, pulling down his gas mask. "Let him up, or he'll pop her, and I'll spray your brain all over his face shield."

My heart is pounding—and not just with the adrenaline-excitement of the situation and the spike of physical activity, but with fear and dread, and the symptoms that accompany post-traumatic stress. The last time I had a shotgun pointed at me, it was in Potter High School, and Derek Burrell was on the other end of it.

I don't move, but I'm not sure how long I can keep it together. I can tell I'm about to lose it.

Unable to catch my breath I can feel myself starting to panic.

"Last chance, nigger lover," he says. "We got the drop on y'all."

His ignorance and racism brings me back from the brink a little, and I can feel my anxiety subside a bit.

"Cap, you okay in there?" the other one says toward the still open door of the hotel room as he too removes his gas mask.

"Rethinking wearing those gas masks, aren't y'all?" I ask.

Merrill steps out of the room with Cap in a chokehold with one arm and his .45 in the hand of the other, which he presses to the base of the neck of the man holding the shotgun on me.

"Who's got the drop on whom?" Merrill says.

I can hear the smile in his voice.

The man holding the gun on me doesn't speak or move.

"We still got two of y'all in our sights," the man holding the gun on Tana says.

"Then it's three to two," Merrill says. "Our way."

"This ain't no game, goddamnit," he says.

"Doesn't matter what you call it," Merrill says, "comes to the same thing. Y'all tried, and you failed. This is over. Only question is *how* over? You want to live to fuck up another day, or you want to die now here in the hallway of the Holiday Inn?"

"We got the drop on y'all," the man over by Tana says.

"We covered that already," Merrill says. "We've got more drop than y'all. Keep up. We're not giving in. No matter what. You might clip the girl. Y'all might even get a round off into John's hard head, but all y'all dying here in this hallway tonight unless you drop your matching little blasters."

"Then I guess we got us a little Mexican standoff," the guy holding the gun to my head says.

"And ain't a Mexican among us," Merrill says. "Ain't that some shit. Wonder where that comes from anyway,

Mexican standoff. One of y'all Google it and see, I'd really like to know."

Merrill's ease and confidence and the amusement in his voice helps to ground me and dissipates my distress.

"It's from the nineteenth century," Tana says. Her voice is weak but grows stronger as she speaks. "I wrote about it in my book. Some people think it had to do with the Mexican-American War or the activities of the post-war bandits. And it means what you think it means—a confrontation between parties where there is no strategy that would give any party a victory."

"Thank you, Ms. Tana," Merrill says. "That's good to know. I love learnin' new shit. Don't you, boys?"

None of them respond.

"Thing is . . ." Merrill says, "that's not what we have here. Our side has a strategy that will lead to victory. And we have all the time in the world. Because the moment I heard your dumb gas-mask-wearing asses out here in the hall I called y'all's coworkers at the station. More cops are on they way right now."

"These are police officers?" Tana asks.

"They not on the clock right now," Merrill says. "In fact, they've ridden way off the reservation but yeah, they cops. Same corrupt motherfuckers who tried to corner up me and Ms. Malia in the parking lot of that little church off 11th Street a few days ago."

The guy Merrill has in a chokehold tries to say something, but it's incomprehensible.

"If I loosen my grip on you, you gonna say something intelligent?" Merrill says.

"He's right," Cap says as Merrill lets off enough for him to speak. "They've got us. We've got no play. Put your weapons down before somebody really gets hurt."

They do as he says.

"We just came to talk to Malia," the man says. "I swear. We wanted to scare her out of doing that march against my boy. That's all. We're not killers. We're not bad men. Just trying to save my son. He's a good man. He doesn't deserve what is happening to him."

"He shot an unarmed kid in his family's own yard," Merrill says. "And no matter what Malia or anyone else does, he'll probably get away with it."

I say, "Have you sent Malia any threatening notes—"

"Notes?" he says in surprise.

"Notes, letters, postcards, telegraphs, telegrams, anything?" I ask.

He shakes his head as best he can with Merrill's huge bicep wrapped around it like a snake on steroids.

"No, nothing like that," he says. "We just wanted to get her to let the pressure off some. Just her presence here in town is drawing so much attention to the case. Don't want my boy to be some national poster child for bad cops."

"Then you should'a raised a better boy," Merrill says. "And made him into a better cop."

25

While Merrill accompanies Malia to a book signing, I meet Trevon Fisher at the Panama City Rescue Mission.

The early May morning is bright and clear and already warm.

Downtown is busy, both its streets and sidewalks buzzing with activity that is completely absent at night.

In operation for over forty-five years, the Panama City Rescue Mission started as a place where the many fishermen passing through Panama City's ports could get a hot meal, fresh clothes, and a warm bed for the night. Now, it is a homeless shelter specializing in an addiction recovery program.

Like me, Trevon Fisher is on administrative leave. He

shows up in street clothes in his own vehicle, a silver GMC truck.

He's meeting me as a favor to a mutual friend of ours. He trusts the friend and the friend trusts me.

"It all happened so fast," he is saying. "From the time I arrived to Sykes falling to the ground dead was, like, less than two minutes."

Carmen Sykes was the homeless man he shot on the west side of the mission after chasing him around the block.

"But," he continues, "that doesn't mean I'm unclear on what happened. He had a gun, and he fired it at me. It wasn't a phone or a toy or a figment of my imagination. It was a real gun, and he shot at me with it."

His mention of a phone makes me think of Boyd Calhoun and his shooting of Antwone Wright.

Boyd's father, Louden, and three other of his fellow PCB police are in custody after storming our hotel hallway with shotguns last night.

"Do you know Boyd Calhoun?" I ask.

He shrugs. "Not really. Know of him. Been around him a few times. Don't really know him. But the bastard is the bane of my existence, I'll tell you that."

"Really? How's that?"

"I'm getting lumped in with him and what they did out there on the beach," he says. "This has nothing to do with that. But the timing . . . with his trial going on and everything . . . My case is getting national attention. Everybody acting like we the same. Well, we ain't. I didn't shoot an unarmed kid in his grandma's backyard. I was being shot at by a suspect, and I returned fire. And if it weren't for Calhoun's case . . . Got this activist in town stirring everybody up . . . gonna do a march. Gonna get my ass hung is what they gonna do."

Evidently, he doesn't know I'm helping with Malia's security, and my highly developed skills as an observer of people tells me I better keep it that way.

"You mind taking me through what happened?" I ask.

He shakes his head. "Sam said you were in a similar situation and you might be able to help."

"Certainly will if I can," I say.

"I'm responding to a call that a white male in a prison uniform is waving a gun around and discharging it in the vicinity of the rescue mission," he says.

I nod.

"When I pull up here," he says, pointing to the side street and parking area around the east side entrance, "he's standing in a small group over there, and he takes off running immediately."

I follow his gaze to where he's pointing.

"Did you see the weapon at the time?"

He shakes his head. "No, he didn't have it out, which is why none of the witnesses on this side testified to seeing it. But he did have one, and he pulled it out as he was running. Another man took off running at the same time, but he didn't match the description, so I just let him go and followed Sykes."

"Did you know him or had you had any dealings with him before that moment?"

He shakes his head.

"I's getting outta my car when he took off, so I get back in and follow him down Allen."

He points down the street we're standing on.

"It's then I first notice the gun—when I'm driving after him. He must have pulled it out somewhere between leaving the mission and cutting through to Wilson because I definitely saw it. I drive down and take a left on East 7th and then another left on Wilson Avenue, figuring he was heading back to the mission. And that's what he's doing. Running down Wilson, the gun in his hand."

"Know what kind of gun it was?" I ask.

"Nickel or stainless revolver of some sort. A .38, maybe. Not sure. But I am sure he had it."

Rather than walking the block, we cross the front of the mission and head down Wilson Avenue to the area where the shooting took place.

"When I got up here, close to the mission, I parked my car and jumped out and started chasing him on foot."

We walk over to the approximate place on Wilson

that he parked his car and turn back and look at the mission from this side.

Large trees line the side dirt lot next to the west side of the mission. A rickety wooden fence frames part of the property. Inside it, there is a storage shed that serves as a pantry right off the back of the kitchen. There's a garden. There's also a random and eclectic assortment of objects, including toys, tires, old vehicles, and a boat.

"I still hadn't drawn my weapon at that point."

"He runs down there to the corner of the fence, crouches behind it and starts firing," he says, pointing to the place near the front part of the lot we had just passed when we walked over here.

I look over to the place where he's pointing.

"There were people around," he says. "Kids. I was afraid someone was going to get hurt or killed. Something took over, and I just started running toward where he was. Still, don't know how I didn't get shot. I thought for sure I would. Figured my car would be all shot up. He fired several rounds. I know people heard it. But . . ."

We walk back down Wilson, which slopes toward Business 98.

"When I reach the corner of the fence here, he's gone," he says. "I can see him disappearing behind the trees over there next to the front mission building. He was sort of hidden behind that first oak tree right there. As I got closer, he started firing at me again, and this time

I fired back. I was trying to just hit his hand, make him drop the gun."

Suddenly I am back in the hallway of Potter High School trying to do the same thing to Derek Burrell.

"Wasn't trying to kill him, but . . . one of the rounds hit him in the head."

He describes Carmen Sykes falling but what I picture is Derek Burrell pitching forward, his shotgun clattering on the hallway floor.

"People were scattering," he is saying. "Running. Hiding behind other trees. I tried to get them to stop, but most of them didn't. When I ran up to the place where Sykes had fallen I saw two things immediately—he was dead, and he didn't have a gun. But he did. I'm telling you he did. I know he did. But . . . I don't know. No one ever testified that he did and no weapon was ever found anywhere. Most of the witnesses vanished and were never seen again. And we have no way to trace them. The few that did stick around and give a statement said since he didn't have a gun the shots they heard must have all been from me. And I understand why they would say that. I do. But . . . I don't know. I just . . . Maybe he didn't have a gun. Maybe I imagined it all. Because not only was no weapon found but no rounds were either. Not a single projectile. Not a single round pulled out of my car or anything else. And I could have sworn I heard glass shattering and bullets ricocheting off the asphalt. That's what makes me doubt myself. It'd be one thing if we just couldn't find the gun, but not to be able to find a single round anywhere . . . Maybe I'm just as guilty as Calhoun. Maybe I deserve all that I'm getting. Maybe I did kill an unarmed civilian just like him."

26

When Merrill and Malia arrive at Books-A-Million, they find protesters out front but none blocking the doors.

Two police cars are parked near the entrance, and two cops are present.

The protesters are assembled to the left of the building, between Toys "R" Us and the bookstore.

"Well, at least it looks like we'll be able to get in," Malia says.

"Could have at the library, you let me make a hole," Merrill says.

"I was concerned who you might make the hole through," she says.

As they get out of the vehicle, Khyree Todd, looking especially like a young Denzel in his gray suit, white shirt, black tie, and flat gray paperboy cap, emerges from the store and walks toward them.

Malia beams, obviously happy to see him.

Merrill says, "Now what're the chances we'd run into him here today?"

"Pretty good," she says. "He's a big-time reader."

"Oh, so anytime anybody show up at the bookstore be a good chance you'll find ol' Khyree?"

"You came," Malia says to Khyree as he approaches.

"Of course," he says. "My favorite author is signing books here today."

"That's so sweet," she says to him, then turning to Merrill, "Isn't that sweet?"

They embrace and kiss.

As they do, Merrill continues to scan the parking lot, paying particularly close attention to the protesters.

"Everything looks so good the way they have it set up inside," Khyree says. "They asked me what you'd like to drink. I had them fix you a coffee and a water. Hope that's okay."

"That's great. Thank you. That's so sweet. Isn't that sweet? Isn't he just the—"

"*Sweetest*," Merrill says.

"Shall we go in?" Malia asks.

Merrill nods.

As the three of them walk toward the entrance to the store, Khyree says, "There's a huge poster of you behind the table where you'll be signing. I was wondering . . . Think they'd let me have it after you're done?"

"I'm sure they will," she says. "They usually offer them to me, and I certainly don't want it. It's so sweet of you to want it. Just the . . . Isn't he just the sweetest?"

"Hands down," Merrill says. "Just the absolute sweetest."

Merrill notices a vehicle with a car cover over it in the parking spot closest to the bookstore. Placing his hand at the small of Malia's back and gently shepherding her in the opposite direction, he guides her well away from the car.

Khyree follows as Merrill knew he would.

As they near the store, the protesters begin to chant.

"Our town is not up to you. Blue lives matter too. What you say is untrue. Blue lives matter too."

The two PCPD patrol cops step over so that they are between the protesters and door where Malia will enter the store.

Malia smiles and nods toward the protesters. "I agree," she says. "All except the untrue part."

"Don't you dare laugh at us," one yells.

"You use tragedies to sell books," another one yells.

"There's blood in your pen and on your hands."

"What you say is untrue. Blue lives matter too."

"All lives matter," Malia yells, trying to start a chant of

her own. "Everybody now— All lives matter. Come on. All lives matter."

Though they look confused, none of the protesters join her.

"No?" she says. "Okay. Well, if you change your mind, I'll be inside signing books. Extra 10 percent off if you bring your protest sign. I especially like the one with my face on the baboon. Zoo lives matter, am I right?"

Khyree holds the door open for her and Merrill ushers her inside.

As he passes by the cops, Merrill asks if they will check the vehicle beneath the car cover.

They nod and say they will, but neither makes a move to do so.

Inside the store, to the right in front of the coffee shop, a long table with a pressed white tablecloth has been set up. Behind it, a padded chair. Behind the chair, the poster of Malia. On top of the table, an assortment of pens is arranged near a paper cup of coffee and a bottle of water.

A long line of customers extending down the center aisle of the store erupts in applause.

So far no sign of the creepy young albino-looking fucker.

Merrill wonders whether that's a good thing or not.

"Thank you," she says. "And thank you all for braving the unpleasantness out front and joining me here today. I look forward to signing my new book for you and meeting you as I do. Let's get started, shall we?"

As she makes her way over behind the table, Tana and Rodney come up from a side aisle with the manager, distraught looks on their faces.

The manager is a short, roundish woman with big bifocals and shiny black hair cut in a bob.

Merrill takes it all in—but far more too—as he continually scans the store, keeping his vision broad and unfocused, alert to any sudden movement or suspicious activity, his hand never far from the .45 on his hip hidden by his sports coat.

"We've got a problem," Rodney says.

"What now?" Malia asks.

"There are no books," Tana says.

"I thought we already confirmed they were here," Malia says.

"We did."

"Y'all did," the manager says.

"Then what's the problem?" Malia asks.

"Apparently someone came in and bought them all last night," the manager says.

"What?"

"Bought every copy they had," Tana says. "With cash so we can't . . . We have no idea who did it."

"Y'all didn't find it suspicious?" Malia asks the manager.

"I wasn't on duty at the time, but the gentleman purchasing the books said he was acting on your behalf and that you planned to surprise everyone who showed up today with a free copy."

"Do you have a description of this man?" Khyree asks.

"A middle-aged white man with long dark hair, a thick mustache, and dark sunglasses," the manager says.

"Sounds like a disguise," Merrill says.

"I'm so sorry that this has happened," the manager says. "The sales clerk who did it feels horrible, but she had no idea it was in any way malicious. She's an innocent victim in this as much as anyone else."

"Well," Malia says, "maybe not quite as much as anyone else."

"I wish there were something we could do," the manager says. "But we're the only new bookstore in town, and there's nowhere to get more copies right away. I checked, and our warehouse in Alabama doesn't even have enough to replace what we had—and it'd take two days to get what they do have here."

"Well, I guess I need to explain to these fine people standing in line what is going on," Malia says.

"I'd be happy to do it if you want me to," the manager says.

"Thank you, but I think it should come from me."

Malia steps over and stands in front of those gathered.

"Ladies and gentlemen, can I have your attention?" Malia says.

But before she can say anything else, a big burst of flame and accompanying whooshing sound draws everyone's attention to the parking lot.

Merrill is suddenly next to Malia, an arm around her.

Everyone begins rushing to the front of the store and the large plate glass windows there to see what's happening.

In the first spot on the left side of the parking lot, the car cover has been removed to reveal that what is actually beneath it is not a vehicle but Malia's books that had been purchased the previous night.

The protesters, who appear as surprised as everyone else about what is happening, begin to cheer.

The hardcover copies of *Shots Fired*, which prominently feature a picture of Malia, are stacked in the shape of a pyramid and engulfed in high flying flames.

Because of the prominence of her picture, it appears that not only her work but Malia herself is being burned in effigy.

27

The last time there was a knock on Merrill's hotel room door, two men with shotguns were standing there. This time it's a brilliant, beautiful doctor—the perfect prescription for the end of a long, difficult day.

He opens the door to see Zaire Bell.

"Decided to surprise you," she says.

"Best surprise ever," he says, wrapping her up in a passionate embrace and pulling her into the room.

Following the incident with Louden Calhoun in the hallway and the book burning at Books-A-Million, PCPD has taken a more active role—with both investigation and protection. Merrill is a little more relaxed, a little more at ease, because there's a uniform in the lobby and at the end of their floor near the elevator.

Beneath her large afro, Za's deep, dark eyes look tired but happy and wanton.

Zaire, Merrill's ever increasingly serious girlfriend, is a doctor at Sacred Heart Hospital in Port St. Joe. She has driven over an hour to get here after a grueling shift and has to be back at the hospital early in the morning. It's an act of extreme selflessness, an expression of love that touches Merrill more than he can say.

She has come straight from the hospital and is still wearing her scrubs and clogs.

How can she smell so good? How is that even possible?

"Can't tell you what it means to me that you drove over to see me," he says.

"I would walk five hundred miles and I would walk five hundred more just to be the girl who collapsed at your hotel door."

"What does *haver* mean?" he says.

"Huh?"

"I've always wondered what *haver* means. 'And if I haver, I'm gonna be the man who's havering to you.'"

"I think it means to babble or talk nonsense."

"My girl's so smart."

"I've got a question for you," she says. "Were there actual Nazis at the book burning today?"

"As a matter of fact there were," he says. "But incognito so I wouldn't shoot they ass."

"Shame."

"Speaking of ass," he says.

"Mine's all yours," she says. "Just as soon as I pee. That was a long ass drive over and I've had to pee since Mexico Beach."

A few minutes later, she emerges from the bathroom naked, her cinnamon body so breathtaking Merrill finds it painful.

As they climb into his bed, she glances over at John's. "Think John and Anna have made love in that one?"

"Fairly certain of that very thing," he says.

"It's interesting to think about," she says. "Of the hundreds of people who've made love in this room, we know at least two."

"Maybe more," Merrill says. "I know a lot of people."

Within moments the two lovers not only have no thoughts of any other people but feel as though there are no other people on the planet.

28

It's late.

Malia and I are in the hotel bar.

We are seated at the far end, as far away from everyone else as we can be—though there are only three other people in the bar, including the bartender.

It's dim and quiet and we're speaking very softly.

I had been out in the hallway when she opened the door and asked me if I'd come down and have a drink with her.

I'm having a purposefully weak vodka and cranberry. She's sipping whiskey.

"No offense to this lovely town," she says, "but I don't want to die in Panama City."

"We're gonna make sure you don't."

"So many days . . ." she says. "So many days I just

wanna pack it all in and go home. But . . . Malik's death has to mean something. Has to. Graham's did—does. He was serving his city honorably, but I've got to . . . It's up to me to make sure Malik's means something."

I nod.

Neither of us says anything for a few moments.

Eventually, I raise my glass and say, "To Malik."

She lifts her whiskey and lightly touches my glass with it. "To Malik."

We each take a sip of our drinks.

"Thank you," she says.

I nod and we fall quiet again.

I get the sense that Malia had been drinking before we came down to the bar, and she seems if not buzzed, well on her way.

"Life is a series of losses," she says. "First Graham, then Malik, now Tana. Hellos and too soon goodbyes. She's gonna be impossible to replace."

"You still have a while," I say. "And why not hire two or three people to replace her?"

"Can't afford two or three," she says. "Hell, havin' a hard time affording her. And I don't have a while. I have virtually no time at all. I think that thing in the hallway with Louden Calhoun and them really shook her up. She gave me a hard deadline of the end of this trip. Don't know what I'm gonna do . . . Irreplaceable. 'Course, it's not an issue if I don't survive this trip."

"You will," I say, trying to sound reassuring but not certain I do.

"I didn't intend any of this," she says after a while. "Didn't ask for it. Or maybe in a way I did. I don't know. But . . . we have to step up, don't we? Take advantage of the opportunities presented to us, right? I could just go home and write books, but . . . I have a voice when so many don't. A responsibility has been entrusted to me. I don't know . . . I'm just . . . Sometimes it feels like too much, like I can't do it. I didn't ask to be a voice within a movement. And damn sure don't want to be a martyr for it. And yet . . . sometimes martyrs are the most important . . . parts of a movement."

I haven't fully realized until this moment just what enormous pressure she is perpetually under.

"I'm not saying I want to die," she says, "so don't let me."

"I won't," I say, adding after a moment, "I'm not going to let anyone else die."

"*Ever*?"

"If I can help it."

"Well, all right then," she says, and lifts her glass. "To defense against the Grim Reaper. Do your best GR. But you gotta get through a Mr. John Jordan."

I smile and we retreat back into our own private silences.

She takes another drink.

I glance at my glass. I've had very little of it. And I feel very good about that.

You have no power over me.

Oh, just you wait. This isn't over yet.

"What was your impression of Trevon Fisher?" Malia asks.

"Seems like a good man and a good cop," I say.

"Think he's tellin' the truth?"

"I think he thinks he is," I say.

"That's not the same thing, is it?" she says.

"All the evidence contradicts his account," I say. "It's not just that there was no gun found, there's no evidence of one. At all. And yet . . . I found myself believing him."

"Believing him or wanting to?" she asks. "In the heat of the moment when you're in the middle of a firefight . . . you can see and hear all sorts of things that just aren't there."

I nod and think about it some more.

"He says he's getting crucified because of the Antwone Wright case and the national attention you and others are bringing to both."

"He's probably right," she says. "And if it's doing so unfairly . . . I hate it. But if he killed an unarmed man with mental illness in cold blood . . . then he deserves more than he's getting."

I'm not sure I agree.

"It's a lot easier when they're defiant, belligerent

assholes like Boyd Calhoun and his crew. Did you hear those motherfuckers are already bonded out?"

I nod.

"They make a third run at me I'm beginning to hope their fate's not decided by the courts."

I shudder at the thought of shooting them or anyone else, and find myself hoping the exact opposite.

The bartender brings Malia another drink. She lifts it and swirls the golden-brown liquid around the tumbler and studies it.

"'Malt does more than Milton can to justify God's ways to man,'" she says.

"I haven't found that to be the case," I say, "so I'll have to respectfully disagree with Mr. Housman. Speaking of God . . . Things seem to be going well with the Reverend Todd."

She laughs. "Sounds funny to call him anything other than Khyree or Young Denzel. I had forgotten he was a man of the cloth. But as far as how things are going . . . he's just a brief and welcome distraction."

I wonder if he knows that.

"He's sweet and we're having a good time," she contin- ues, "but I leave soon and there's no room in my life for . . . well, much of anything . . . so . . ."

I nod.

"I wish your friend was available," she adds. "I could

make room in my life for him. I'd be like . . . *shee-it* . . . fuck the movement, I'm takin' Merrill home."

"Dr. King would've done the same in your shoes," I say.

"Maybe not, but Coretta damn sure would have. Promise you that. Sister be talkin' 'bout 'Call me Coretta Scott Monroe.'"

"Speaking of the Kings," I say, "I've been looking into the attempts made on you and . . . Atlanta definitely feels different from the other two."

"Y'all 'bout convinced me the other two were legit, but no way anyone'll ever make me think Atlanta was anything but random."

"I'd agree completely," I say, "if it weren't for the post-card. And yet . . . Tana seems to think that unlike the others it came after the incident not before it."

"He sent me a warning after the fact?" she says. "What's the point in that?"

I shrug. "Maybe to just take credit for it. The way Zodiac did. Read something in the newspaper or hear about it and act like you did it."

"But what's the point—in my case?"

"I'm not sure. Could be the same thing. Except whereas Zodiac was trying to strike fear in a city, this guy's only trying to frighten you."

"You think if I packed it all in tonight and went home, he'd leave me alone?"

"Depends."

"On what?"

"The nature of his obsession. Is it really about the work or is he fixated on you?"

"The work, surely. I hadn't even thought about the possibility of it being me."

"Probably difficult for him to differentiate between the two."

"Then I'd say I'm fucked."

29

I spend the rest of the night in the hallway thinking about the attempts on Malia's life in Chicago, Atlanta, and Madison.

I think about the postcards, the warnings they contain, the attempts, going over them step by step, detail by detail. I think about the Atlanta postcard coming in after the fact.

I think about the actions of Louden Calhoun and Jerry Edwards and the fact that Jerry is from Chicago.

I think through the actions of the protesters at the library and the bookstore and who might have purchased all the copies of *Shots Fired* and burned them in the parking lot.

Finally, I try to assess future threats, pressing myself to imagine new types of attempts that haven't been employed yet—and I am struck by a simple and obvious one.

When Merrill relieves me the next morning, I go straight downstairs and begin to sift through the mail bins—but not before I ask him if what he's whistling is "I'm Gonna Be" by the Proclaimers.

"'When I wake up . . .'" he begins to sing. "'. . . I'm gonna be the man who wakes up next to her.'"

A short while later, as I am kneeling down behind the counter humming "500 Miles" while looking through the mail, I see Rodney arrive from wherever he has been the entire night.

He glances around nervously as he enters the lobby in the same clothes he had on the previous day, but doesn't see me as he quickly rushes by on his way to the elevators.

When he is gone, I gather all the gifts into a single bin and head out to my vehicle with them.

For the next few hours, instead of sleeping I drive to nearby stores—Target, Walmart, CVS, Walgreens, Books-A-Million—trying to determine where the gifts had come from and even repurchasing some of them.

On my way back to the hotel, I call Sam Michaels and ask for her help with the FDLE lab.

It's just a theory and it may be nothing, but I feel as though I have to try everything, test every idea.

She agrees to help and so I reroute and head to the post office before returning to the hotel.

When I arrive back at the hotel, I walk in with the bin that now includes some repurchased gifts and replace it behind the counter.

I've only gotten a few steps back into the lobby when I see Tana coming over from the elevators.

"You heading up?" she asks.

I nod.

"You mind helping me carry the mail?"

"Not at all," I say.

As we go behind the front desk for the bins of mail, the clerk shoots me a quizzical look, but doesn't say anything.

When we are in the elevator with the luggage cart full of mail bins of letters and packages and presents, I ask how she is doing.

"I'm okay," she says. "That was . . . I thought for sure I was going to die. I mean, I knew you and Merrill would do all you could to protect me, but . . . I just thought we were too outnumbered."

"Always outnumbered," I say. "Always outgunned."

"I'm still jumpy."

"Malia said you turned in your notice with a more definitive deadline."

"*Deadline*," she says. "Interesting choice of words."

"Was it the experience in the hallway that made you go ahead and—"

"Yeah, but not in the way you probably think," she says. "I didn't do it because I'm scared. I mean, I am, but that's not why I did it. I did it because in that moment when I thought I was going to die I looked at my life and didn't like what I saw. It's not even my life. It's Malia's. I'm living her life or helping her live hers, not even living my own. Answering her mail, writing her books and speeches, planning her events, taking care of her travel and schedule and . . . everything. I have no life. And I don't want to die without getting one. So I'm going for it. Gonna write my books. Gonna try my hand at speaking and . . . well, living."

"Good for you," I say. "That's great."

"Thanks. I'm excited. And terrified."

"Speaking of Malia's schedule," I say, "what do we have today."

I'm hoping to get a few hours' sleep before we have to be somewhere.

"That ridiculous debate with that absurd old man," she says. "The only good thing about it is we don't have to do anything for it. Just show up and debate. He's taking care of everything else."

"Yeah," I say, "I'm not sure that's such a good thing at all."

30

"This is a setup," Malia says when we walk into the side door of the Martin Theater.

We are standing at ground level. To our left is the stage a few feet above our heads. To our right are the rows and rows of built-in theater seating rising at a steep incline to the back row at the top of the building some forty feet above where we are now.

Jerry Edwards is standing on the stage with the help of his forearm crutches in front of two podiums between two large American flags in an ill-fitting navy-blue suit, white shirt, and too long red tie. The entire platform and backdrop is decorated in red, white, and blue, looking more like a political rally than a social policies debate.

"The son of a bitch," Tana says next to me.

Only angry, white, older supporters of Jerry Edwards are in the audience of the partially filled theater.

"He only advertised it to his supporters," Malia says. "Where's Jerry? This is the very thing he's supposed to be . . . He should've been on top of this."

"And the media, of course," Tana says, nodding toward the TV news camera crews set up on either side of the front.

A historical landmark on Harrison Avenue in Downtown Panama City for over seven decades, the Martin Theater was originally the Ritz Theater, a movie house owned by a Columbus, Georgia-based cinema chain, when it first opened its doors in 1936.

During its early days, the Ritz was visited by celebrities such as Clark Gable, Constance Bennett, Michael O'Shea, William Boyd, and Bill Elliot.

In the 50s, the Martin family purchased and remodeled the Ritz chain, replacing the original marquee with one that still stands out front to this day.

Until 1978, the Martin Theater was a movie house, and in fact, I had seen a few movies here when I was a kid. After it closed, it was left vacant except for the short time it was a shooting gallery, until 1987, when the Downtown Improvement Board purchased it and restored it with the help of state funds.

Reopening in November of 1990, the remodeled and

renovated theater has been hosting everything from concerts to plays to local dance recitals ever since.

"Can you delay it for a few minutes?" Khyree asks.

Malia nods. "Why?"

"Give me a few minutes to round up some of my congregation to join us," he says.

"I can put out an invite on social media too," Tana says.

"Do it," Malia says. "Might as well keep doin' Jerry's damn job for him."

Climbing the stairs with me and Merrill in front and back of her, Malia walks over and shakes Jerry Edwards's hand to boos from the crowd.

"We're gonna need a few minutes," she says. "My security team needs to check out the building and I'm gonna run to the restroom before we begin."

"You nervous, Malia?" he asks, a self-satisfied smirk on his wrinkled face.

"*Yeah*," she says with exaggerated sarcasm, "that's it, Jerry."

Roughly ten minutes later when the debate begins, very few additional people have joined the audience.

With Malia and Jerry each standing behind one of the two podiums, Malia on the left, Jerry on the right, Jerry starts to say something, but Malia stops him.

"Before we begin," she says, "I'd like to say that I'm happy to be here with you tonight. Jerry has been begging me to debate him for a very long time, and I finally agreed. In fact, I agreed to everything Jerry wanted. He picked the place and time and topic—which he still hasn't revealed to me."

"It's a surprise," he says, and gives the audience a wink and a big smile.

"I'm fine with all that," she continues. "And I don't labor under any delusion that anyone attending tonight is open enough to have their mind changed. Fine. But I do insist on civility and respect and common courtesy. I will give it and I expect it—from Mr. Edwards and from you. If this devolves into anything less than that I will judge this exercise a waste of all our time and will put an end to it. Thank you."

"I'm glad you demand respect," Jerry says, "because that's our subject matter for tonight. Should our country's citizens—*all* our country's citizens—stand for the national anthem?"

"Wow," Tana says to me. "Whatta bastard. This is just red meat for his followers. He's tossing out bloody chum behind his boat. There's nothing she can say that will convince this crowd of anything and he knows it."

She and I are standing in the wings, watching Malia as she speaks. It's dim back here and dusty, but we can see if anyone approaches Malia from the front or back. Merrill is set up on the opposite side doing the same thing.

"I'll go first," Edwards says.

"Wait," Malia says. "You're a participant in and the moderator of the debate?"

"Yeah," he says, with another wink and a smile to his audience, "I'm a great multitasker."

The crowd cheers for him.

"My opening statement is simple," Edwards says. "My son spilled his blood on a foreign battlefield fighting for this great country and I was wounded as a police officer serving and protecting the great citizens of this great country here at home, and it is goddamn disrespectful to both of us and every other man and woman in this history of our country for some overpaid grown man who makes millions playing with a fuckin' ball to kneel during our nation's song. Period. The end. Enough said. It's a shame. It's a sham. It's a disgrace. And it's the height of disrespectful."

The crowd erupts in cheers and applause, many of them standing and whistling and yelling.

It takes a while for the audience to sit and quiet back down, but when they do, Edwards looks over at Malia, giving her a nod and the lift of his hand to signify it is her turn should she dare to go.

"I want to thank you and your son for your service," she says. "*Thank you* is woefully inadequate given the sacrifice you both have made, but it is sincere and deeply, profoundly genuine."

As she is speaking, Edwards is nodding his head and looking like *Yeah, yeah, whatever, get on with it so you can say what you really want to*, but when she doesn't say anything else he seems at a loss.

"That it?" he asks.

She nods.

"I know you have strong opinions on this issue," he says.

"They can wait," she says. "We'll get to them. I don't want to take away from my appreciation of your and your son's service by saying anything else at this time."

Like Edwards, the crowd doesn't seem to know quite how to react.

"Well, okay, ah ..." he begins, "far better men than the ones kneeling have died for the flag and that anthem and for what this country stands for. You dishonor them and your country by not standing. The only reason they take a knee, the only reason they are able to, is because our flag, our anthem, our country doesn't mean to them what it should. You can't love something and disrespect it. You can't love something and trash it. You just can't. Kneeling while our national anthem is played is unpatriotic and shows you don't love your country and I'd like to suggest that if you don't love this country find one you do."

Slowly, but steadily, members of Khyree's congregation and Malia's social media followers in the area begin to trickle in and sit down.

"I stand for the anthem," Malia says. "Always have. But I support those who in peaceful protest of police shooting of unarmed citizens take a knee. And I'll tell you why. Peaceful protest has a rich tradition in this great country as a way of drawing attention to and actually changing things for the better. And this is a great country, but it's not a perfect one, not a sinless one. And loving your country doesn't mean being dishonest about what some in it have done or still do. That's denial—and whether in a family or a church or in a government, it's dangerous and destructive. But this isn't about our country so much as it is about the protest of unarmed citizens—many of them completely innocent, good, upstanding young men—being murdered and nothing being done about it. You can disagree with the way in which the protest is being carried out, but it is disingenuous to say it's about something that it is not. It does not signify disrespect. It is not unpatriotic. It has nothing whatsoever to do with the flag or our troops and to say it does is not only to lie but to make civil discourse impossible—which is why it's done, of course. How can anyone say they're in favor of police shooting unarmed citizens? So cynical politicians and pundits say untrue and outrageous things to change the conversation and rile up their supporters about issues that have nothing to do with what's really being protested."

"The fact remains," Edwards says, "that they are

taking a knee during the anthem—not the coin toss, not the prayer, not during the game, but during the anthem."

"So you don't approve of when they are peacefully protesting, say that," Malia says. "Hell, even offer alternatives, but don't claim it's something that it's not. Again, these are peaceful protests about a very specific issue—police shooting of unarmed citizens. It's a healthy expression of an extraordinary freedom we have. That's the thing about freedom—it has to apply to everyone or it's not freedom. The freedoms that our troops fight to protect include peaceful protest of our government or our police or anything else we want to protest. You're saying that by taking a knee during the anthem someone is dishonoring those who serve. I say just the opposite. Those who serve, those who fight against oppressive regimes around the world where individuals don't have the right to protest do so to keep us free to protest, to stand up to power, to remain truly free. Exercising our freedoms is honoring not dishonoring them. Your side is the first to say 'Don't tread on me. Fuck the government. I'm free, white, and twenty-one and I'll do whatever the fuck I please.' But you don't want those same freedoms afforded to all citizens."

"You show respect for that freedom," Edwards says, "the symbols of that freedom. You honor that freedom not by protesting it, but by standing and honoring it and protesting something else."

"Right now you are expressing your freedom," Malia says to Edwards. "Would you still be free if someone came in and told you how you could do it—or when or where?"

"I'm not saying these millionaire ball players aren't free to do what they're doing," he says. "I'm not trying to stop them. I'm using my freedom to disagree with them."

"If that's all you and those on your side of this issue were doing, that would be one thing, but that's not all you're doing. Those protesting are doing so peacefully and respectfully. Are those of you protesting the protesters being as peaceful and respectful? If so, fine. Great. All good. But if you in any way lie or distort what the protest is really about or in any way try to diminish their freedom to peacefully protest, then you, sir, are the ones being disrespectful and dishonest."

Edwards starts to say something, but Malia holds up her hand.

"Can I just ask you one question?" she says. "Just one, and I'd really challenge everyone here to think about it, I mean really think about it. Well, maybe a few questions. The first— Does someone kneeling in the most peaceful of protests during the national anthem bother you more than an unarmed citizen being killed by the police? Which have you been more vocal about? Which have you spent the most time on?"

The room goes silent.

Malia waits but Edwards doesn't say anything.

"Let me ask you another question. What would you do if it were your unarmed children being gunned down? Practicing compassion means we put ourselves in the place of another and feel what they are feeling. Can we do that? Can you honestly say that if it was innocent, unarmed white kids being killed you would do something as restrained and dignified and respectful as taking a knee?"

Edwards says, "Deal with the individual cop who shot someone, don't disrespect all cops and our country."

"The problem has been objectively proven to be systemic," she says. "It's not one cop. It's a racial bias that pervades our culture. It's an issue that has to be addressed in all police departments, all law enforcement agencies in the entire country."

"You're not giving cops enough credit," he says. "They're the good guys. You're acting as if they're the criminals."

"That's not true at all," she says. "Most cops are good guys. Some of them are actually great guys. And, like in the general population, some are not good guys and shouldn't be in law enforcement. And I've never said anything different. That goes back to what I was saying earlier about changing what someone has said or done. Win the argument with the facts, with only dealing with what the person on the other side of the debate has actually said or done. If a person protests police shootings of unarmed citizens, don't say he's doing something else. It's that simple."

"Bottom line, it's disrespectful," he says. "It dishonors the men and women who died and the country they died for to give you the right to make millions playing ball."

"I wonder how many of you here tonight find kneeling during the anthem disrespectful, but have no problem waving and wearing the Confederate flag—a flag that is in direct opposition to the *United* States flag. In the same way a Nazi flag is. Of course, in this great country you're free to wave or wear any flag you like— even those that stand for things that go against our country's flag. Absolutely free to do so. All I'm wondering is if you find it disrespectful."

"That's a great point for our side," Edwards says. "Your side does find the Confederate flag disrespectful and offensive and are demanding that we take it and other statues and monuments down in the public square. While these football players are doing what they're doing in the public square."

"That's a total false equivalency," Malia says. "What's being taken down are state-sponsored symbols of slavery and oppression and a group of states trying to defeat or end the United States. Individuals are allowed to wear or display any Confederate symbol they want to—in the public square. Some are doing so here tonight. There are tags on cars parked right outside of here—in the public square. When we have our march on Thursday, there will be counter protesters waving Confederate flags in our faces and on the street corners—in the public square. It's the difference in individuals' rights and freedoms versus state-sponsored items and actions that hinder those freedoms. And that's all the difference in the world."

"Well," Edwards says, "I still say kneeling during the anthem is disrespectful to our country and our troops and you're not going to change my mind on that."

"Never thought I was," she says. "You asked for this debate, not me. You chose the topic, not me."

"I'll just close with one last question," he says, "and we can all go home. You asked me a question and you asked me to really think about and consider it, so I'm asking you to do the same. Will you?"

She nods. "I will. You have my word on that."

"How can a woman who claims to be against police shootings be employing a police officer who shot and killed an unarmed kid in a school shooting just a few weeks ago?"

My heart starts pounding and my clammy skin breaks out into an ice-cold sweat.

"I'm not," she says. "I would never—"

"You damn sure are," he says, relishing every second of this thing he's saved for his final point of the night. "Sheriff's Investigator John Jordan shot and killed Derek

Burrell, a student at Potter High School just over two weeks ago. How can you defend that? How can you be employing the very kind of cop you say you're fighting against? Is it because he shot and killed a white kid? Is that it?"

31

"He wasn't unarmed," Merrill is saying.

"It doesn't matter," Malia says.

The three of us are standing backstage at the Martin in a seating area of old mismatched couches and chairs, surrounded by the dusty props from decades of plays and productions.

"It was an active school shooter situation," Merrill says. "The guy was firing at John with a shotgun."

"You think the details matter?" she asks. "Are you really that naive?"

"It was a clean shoot. He was cleared by a thorough FDLE investigation."

"You should have told me," she says. "You didn't because you knew I'd never have said yes."

Rodney walks up.

"Not now," she says.

"The news is reporting that the family of the victim is suing John for wrongful death and that it wasn't even his jurisdiction that it happened in."

"Oh, my God," she says, glancing from Merrill to me and back again with a look of hurt, anger, and betrayal. "In a single night you've managed to destroy years of incredibly hard work and—" Turning to Rodney she asks, "Are there any news crews still here? I need to put out a statement as quickly as possible."

"I'll work with Tana to get some back," he says. "Want her to craft a statement?"

"Yes and then she and I can tweak it."

She turns back to us. "Do you have any idea what you've done? Do you really disdain the work we're doing that much? Did you sabotage it on purpose or are you just this . . . I'm sorry. I'm hurt and angry—for the setback of the cause far more than any personal setback for me. I like you two. I do. And I've been very happy with your work. It's just . . . This is catastrophic for us. It will be used by every critic and opponent of our cause from now on."

"I'm very sorry," I say. "This is all my fault. I assumed you knew. I walk around thinking everybody does. Figured you would have read about it in the papers or seen it on the TV news. I should have made sure you did. Make a statement. Make a show of firing me, though I'm not actually working for you. But keep Merrill on. You need protecting. You need him. How catastrophic would it be to the movement if something happened to you?"

"I can't. I just . . . There's no way. Y'all have left me no choice. Just remember that when we have to say the things we do about you. This could've all been prevented if you had just been honest upfront. And as hurt and disappointed in you both as I am, what I will have to say and do is not personal. It's not payback. It's necessary to salvage what we can of our work from the damage you've done. I've got to go."

She turns and walks away.

I apologize again to her but she doesn't acknowledge it.

Merrill and I are alone in the large open space, surrounded by the props of pretend in an all-too-real situation.

I shake my head and blink my stinging eyes. "I'm so sorry man."

"For what?" he asks, seeming genuinely perplexed.

"For all this," I say. "But mostly for what this will do to your agency."

"You haven't done anything wrong," he says. "Not at Potter High that day and not in any of this."

"I'm not sure about that, but—"

"I am."

"But that has nothing to do with the fallout, the . . ."

"Don't care about any of that," he says. "Got nothing

to do with me. Got no control over it. Always more or different work to do."

"You did this to help me and it is hurting you."

"I look hurt to you?" he says. "Look like I care? I wasn't helping you. You were helping me. And we were both helping her, and if she can't see that . . . nothing left for us to do . . . 'Cept maybe . . ." he adds as if something has just occurred to him, ". . . put out a statement of my own. Yeah, think I will. Walk out there and when they point their cameras at me and ask me their questions, I'a blast they ass with some cold hard truth."

32

"Hey," Anna says as I ease into bed beside her.

"Hey."

"How are you?"

"Before this moment, not so good, but things are definitely improving."

She slides over into my arms and we hold each other for a long, wordless moment.

"I'm so sorry that happened," she says eventually.

We slide our faces just far enough back to see each other in the dim room.

"So so sorry," she continues. "I didn't know anything about it until your dad called to see if I had heard from you. He wants you to call him. Said it didn't matter how late. He's worried about you. It's very sweet."

"I'll call him in the morning," I say. "I'm sure he's asleep by now."

"I'm not sure he'll be able to sleep until he hears from you."

"Okay. I'll call him tonight."

"Tell me how you really are first," she says.

"I'm sure you know."

"I think I can guess," she says. "Want me to try—see how well I know you?"

"Sure."

"I bet you are extremely embarrassed," she says. "You don't like attention on yourself and you absolutely despise negative publicity. It makes you want to disappear, hide out here from the world for a while. In fact, I'd say that's what you were already doing. It's the reason you're not back at work yet. And you had planned to stay here but Merrill pulled you back out into the world, and then this. Right so far?"

I nod.

"Attention makes you feel self-conscious and embarrassed but negative attention intensifies that by a billion," she says. "But you also feel guilty. You still feel guilty about what happened to Derek Burrell."

"Not what happened to him," I say. "What I did to him."

"But you don't just feel guilty about Derek, you also

now feel guilty about all this—and how you think it impacts both Malia and the work she's doing and Merrill and his agency."

"I'd say you know me pretty damn well," I say.

"Oh, I'm not done," she says. "You feel guilty for how this will affect me and the girls too, how it might impact your ability to provide and care for us."

"Too true."

"But that's just the big overriding feelings," she says. "Beneath them is the frustration you feel at not being able to finish the job—to protect Malia and to figure out who's trying to kill her. Underneath everything else I'd say that's eating away at you—maybe just small bites now, but as time passes it will become bigger and bigger bites."

I think about what she has said—how true it all is, how fortunate I am to have a wife who knows me so well and cares so deeply for me.

"Am I right?"

"You know you are."

"All of which is why you absolutely positively cannot hide out here from the world and you absolutely positively must keep working to protect Malia and find out who's trying to kill her. You have to. Don't get me wrong— as much as I hate the circumstances, I'm thrilled to have you back in our bed tonight. And I'm looking forward to seeing more of you and having you around more, but come tomorrow you have to get back out there—see and be seen, and stop an important messenger from being silenced."

33

Despite what Anna said I needed to do, I lie low for the next few days.

I spend time with my girls—Anna, Johanna, and Taylor.

I rest and relax and read.

I catch up on some much needed sleep.

And I avoid the local news.

"We love you bein' here with us, Daddy," Johanna says.

"I love being here with you," I say. "It's my favorite thing."

We are inside a sheet and blanket tent that encompasses most of the living room.

"Yeah," Taylor says. "Now keep reading."

We are lying down, our heads propped up on pillows, Johanna on one side, Taylor on the other, and I'm reading to them—a book that Taylor finds far more interesting than Johanna.

"Can I read it to her?" Johanna asks.

"Sure," I say.

I pass the small book off to her and we swap spots.

She starts reading immediately, her sweet little voice intense and animated.

"You're such a good reader," I say. "I'm so proud of you."

"Shhh," Taylor says, lifting her little finger to her lips. "Let her keep reading."

"Thank you, Daddy," Johanna says between sentences, her reading becoming even more animated.

Eventually, Anna slides into the tent with us. I turn on my side and she spoons me.

"You're such a good reader, sweet girl," she whispers loud enough for Johanna to hear but not disturb her performance.

Wrapping her arms around me, she caresses and rubs and pats me tenderly. I can feel her breath on the back of my neck and occasionally the brush of her lips as she kisses and heals me.

Outside this tent the world seems to be losing its mind. Selfishness and shallowness is celebrated. Tribalism and cynical side-choosing is on the rise. And there's a vast vacuous void of mature and moral leadership.

Inside this tent God is in her heaven and everything is right with the world.

And right now I never want to leave the world of this tent.

34

"I know it could be completely temporary, but so far all the power is still gone," I'm saying to Dave Lloyd.

I'm sitting at my desk in my library Skyping with Dave.

The door is closed, the room dim and quiet, the flicker of candlelight causing shadows to dance on the ceiling above my altar.

All along the plan has been for Dave to see me in person as often as possible while he's in the States, then continue via Skype once he's in Japan. However, since I'm back in Wewa and not wanting to get out he suggested we Skype, which, among other things, will let me know what it will be like when it's our only option.

"I've never had an experience quite like this," I say.

"Never anything close to this really. And like I said I'm acutely aware it could be temporary, but it's just as true now when I have a lot of idle time on my hands as it was when I was busy with the case—which I find encouraging."

"As you should," he says.

"And I keep thinking . . . If I truly were an alcoholic, could the power go out of it for any amount of time?"

"It's an interesting question," he says. "I've worked with people who abused alcohol for a very long time and just stopped one day—no AA, no program, no detox, no nothing—and never went back to it. They and everyone around them thought they were alcoholics—and maybe they were—but maybe they abused alcohol instead of being addicted to it. I've worked with people who've attended AA and stayed sober for years and years and then went back to drinking and drank themselves to death. People are different. We are mysterious and idiosyncratic and as much as we know about addiction there is much we don't understand. I hope the days of alcohol being an issue for you are over for good, but only time will truly tell and I think you need to move forward with extreme caution."

"I know. And I feel like I am. But I'm also counting on you for feedback and accountability where that's concerned."

"That you're open to that is a very good sign," he says.

"I'm not trying to deceive myself or fool anyone," I say. "I don't mind getting back in AA and working the steps and my recovery if need be. But . . . obviously I'd be thrilled if it was a non-issue."

I find the Skype counseling interesting. It's not as odd or off-putting as I thought it might be. After a short while it's almost as if we're face-to-face in the same room, and it gives me hope for when he's back in Japan.

AFTER MY SESSION WITH DAVE, I call an old AA buddy of mine, Stan, with over thirty years' sobriety and share with him what I've been experiencing and thinking and feeling and talking to Dave about.

"It's all bullshit," he says.

I figured this would be his reaction, which was part of the reason I called him.

"Do you know how much money I'd have if I had a dollar for every time an alcoholic told me they really weren't an alcoholic and didn't need AA or a sponsor or anything anymore?"

"A lot?" I say.

"You think this is funny?" he says.

"I wasn't making light of your point," I say.

"The oldest and best trick in the devil's playbook is to convince an addict that he's not an addict. *Boom*. His work is done. You're being deceived by the devil. This—whatever you're going through right now—is temporary. You're gonna drink again. You're gonna get drunk again. You're gonna fuck up your life again. You need to find a meeting right now. You need to get rid of this stinking thinking and get your head right before it's too late."

"You may be right," I say. "It could all be bullshit and I could be the most deceived individual on the planet. I'm not saying I'm not."

"And that makes you feel better about yourself, doesn't it?" he says. "Makes you believe you're different, right? You tell yourself since you're not defensive about it, since you're willing to admit you could be wrong that *that* actually makes you right. You're on a dangerous path my friend. One that leads to destruction. I'm begging you to jump off it as fast as you can. Find a meeting. Get back in the program. Work the steps. Your soul depends on it."

35

Merrill and I are playing basketball at the old gym on Main Street.

I hadn't wanted to come, but didn't feel as though I could say no to anything Merrill asks of me right now.

The old redbrick and wood floor gymnasium is hot—stiflingly so.

There is no air-conditioning, and though we have the doors propped open, very little fresh air blows in, and even that which does is hot.

We played in this gym as kids, and I always feel nostalgic when I'm back in it as an adult.

The ancient hardwoods, the antique metal scoreboard mounted high up on the cinder block wall, the short, wooden pullout bleachers, the distinct smell of decades of basketball played here—all conspire to cause in me a kind of homesickness for the past and an intense appreciation for the present.

We are just shooting around now, warming up before we play. We each have our own ball and are getting our own rebounds, dribbling around and taking shots in concentric half-circles expanding out from the goal.

"Sorry again for costing you that job," I say. "And any other damage I caused. I appreciate what you were doing for me."

"Your ass best not apologize to me again, John," he says. "We've covered this shit. You didn't cost me anything. *You* were helping me, doing *me* a favor. Malia was wrong to let us go. I just hope she lives long enough to regret it."

I nod, continuing to dribble around and shoot.

He shakes his head. "Can't make her let us protect her," he says.

"No, but she can't stop us from still trying to," I say. "I'm still investigating. Have some ideas, may even have a plan or two. Waiting for a little more info to come in."

"Let me know what you need," he says, "how I can help."

"Will do. One of my ideas is out there. One of my plans is pretty radical. Want to make sure I know more before I go much further down certain roads."

He's about to respond when two of the players from

the high school basketball team walk in carrying their shoes and balls.

They are the two best players on Wewa's team. Rico, the tall black kid, has length and good footwork in the paint, and Stockton, the squat, muscular white kid, has speed and phenomenal handles.

"How much longer y'all gonna be?" Rico asks.

Rico is six-two and too skinny, his immature body yet to completely fill out. The scraggly goatee on his pointy chin makes him look like a boyish black Satan.

"Just got here," Merrill says.

"So not much longer," he says, and he and Stockton laugh.

"Y'all welcome to the other end," Merrill says, "or if y'all can beat us, we'a leave and let you young studs have the whole gym to yourselves."

I do not feel like playing these young, quick, athletic kids, and hope they will just take the other end of the gym.

"We like this end," Stockton says.

He has thick calves and the build of a fireplug.

"But we don't want to get shot over it," Rico says, glancing over at me.

Stockton finds that comment especially amusing and fist bumps Rico as they laugh and carry on obnoxiously.

"Wanna play for this end, then?" Merrill asks.

"We're not so sure y'all should be playing each other, let alone real ballers like us," Rico says.

"Suit yourselves."

"But we *do* want this end," Stockton says.

"One way to get it," Merrill says.

"Tell you what," Rico says, "since we don't want to be responsible for hurting a couple of old men . . . and we don't want his ass to shoot us when y'all start losing . . . why don't we shoot for it?"

Merrill smiles.

Though these cocky little kids are underestimating us, they could probably beat us in a full court game. And even though a half-court game of two-on-two would be challenging, I believe with my shooting and Merrill's size and strength and presence in the paint we can beat them two out of three times most any day of the week. But a shooting competition . . . We've been playing decades longer than them. The only advantage they have on us is their youth—an advantage they forfeit in a shootout, where there is little to no running, and skill, not stamina, is the test.

"We could be down with that," Merrill says, "but let's don't just do a single shot. That's too easy. Let's do a three-point shootout."

"Oh hell yeah," Rico says.

"But not just for choice of end of the gym," Merrill says. "Loser leaves."

"That's good with us," Stockton says. "I'm sure y'all don't mind going home. Almost your bedtime anyway, isn't it?"

"It will truly be a pleasure to take your milk money," Merrill says.

A three-point shootout starts with a player in each corner and proceeds around the arc of the three-point line in the five main shooting spots. When a player makes a shot in one spot, he or she advances to the next one. The two players are headed in opposite directions from each other and cross paths twice in the game. Once a player reaches the opposite corner, he or she starts over again. Whoever makes it back to his or her corner first wins. In the two-player version of the competition, one player shoots and the other rebounds, switching with each other every time someone misses.

I begin in one corner with Rico in the opposite, Merrill and Stockton beneath the goal to rebound.

"Ready?" Merrill asks Rico.

"Oh, I'm ready," he says. "Better be askin' him."

"He's ready," Merrill says without even looking over at me.

"Then let's *go*," Rico says, and takes his first shot.

He rushes his shot and it clangs off the flat iron of the back of the rim.

I take my time, line up my shot, bend and push up with my knees, extend my arm up, and follow through with my hand. The ball spins backwards in a high arc and falls straight through the goal without touching it, sitting in the net for a moment as it spins.

I jog over to the next spot as Merrill grabs the ball when it comes out of the net and passes it so that it arrives at the same time I do.

I do the same thing from that spot and so does Merrill.

And again.

I've made three shots before Rico and Stockton, who are having to switch positions with every miss, have made one.

They continue to rush their shots, growing more frustrated with every miss.

My fourth shot rims out and Merrill and I switch positions.

Merrill makes his first shot from the spot of my first miss and advances to the corner that Rico and Stockton are still stuck in.

But just before Merrill arrives, Stockton makes the corner shot and advances out of it.

Merrill makes his first shot in the corner but misses the second one to start the trip back around the arc.

We switch places.

I make the corner shot and get to the second position from it just as Rico is leaving it.

I make the shot there and advance to the very top of the key where Stockton is shooting.

As he misses and he and Rico trade places, I make the shot and advance to the next to last position.

"Da-umn," Merrill says. "You loudmouth little fuckers just got lapped. Played a lot of these over the years. Only seen that happen a time or two."

Rico misses his shot, runs up and catches the long rebound, and slings the ball at the backboard.

As Stockton runs up the ball, cussing Rico while he does, I miss my next shot and Merrill and I trade positions.

"Come on," Rico yells to Stockton. "Catch up to him. Don't let them finish before we even get around the first corner."

But Stockton misses it.

Merrill makes his and advances into the corner we began in for the win.

He shoots.

The ball goes long and careens off the far side of the rim and launches into the stands. I run it up and dribble back to the corner where I started.

Pausing a moment to focus, I take my time and put up my shot.

It rattles around inside the rim a little but goes in for the win—all this as Rico and Stockton have yet to make the wing three on this side.

"Game," Merrill says.

"FUCK," Stockton screams as he throws the ball toward the other end of the gym.

"Should've played us two-on-two," Merrill says.

"It's not too late," Rico says. "We can—"

"Yes it is," Merrill says. "Now get the fuck out of our gym you ignorant, cocky little fucks."

"We'll just play on the other end and not bother y'all," Rico says.

"You had the chance to do that," Merrill says. "You didn't take it. You had to be badasses. And I might even have let that slide, but your partner here's ignorant ass gonna say some shit about John shooting somebody and pissed me off. So go on and get the fuck up out of our gym. And if I ever hear any shit about anybody shootin' anybody again I'm gonna put my hightop up your ass."

"He was just—" Rico begins.

In a low, particularly menacing voice, Merrill says not sings, "R-E-S-P-E-C-T. Y'all go find out what that shit means to me. Now get. This a men-only gym right now."

36

Sam Michaels's call wakes me the next morning.

"You were right," she says. "The lab found potassium cyanide in the box of milk chocolate macaroons."

"Really?"

"Yep."

"It's odorless and tasteless," she says. "It's a white powder that is mixed with a small amount of water and injected into the chocolate. And it would only take a little. It's very powerful. It would take just a few drops of the mixture to do the deed. The killer would have to be very careful not to touch it because it can be absorbed through the skin. He'd have to be careful not to inhale the powder either. Cyanide compounds are used in metal plating and jewelry making and are readily available. Hell, you can order them over the Internet."

"What about any of the other boxes of chocolates? Was it found in any of them?"

"Just that one so far," she says. "Any idea who sent it to her?"

"No, but it was hand-delivered, not mailed, and the only place I could find that carries that exact box is Target. Of course, he could've ordered it online along with the cyanide compound."

"Are there security cameras in the lobby where it was dropped off?"

"I looked through them but they weren't very helpful. If someone comes in the front door and leaves a package on the counter on that far end, they can't be seen. Unless someone comes to the center of the counter, lifts their head slightly and holds what they're carrying up a little, it's very difficult to make out. I was able to make out a few people dropping letters or packages off, but I didn't recognize any of them, and no one delivered a box of milk chocolate macaroons."

"Do you think this is all the work of the same killer?" she asks. "It's rare to have the same person use a truck, a knife, a gun, and now poison. What kind of mind must he have? What kind of killer must he be?"

"Opportunistic," I say. "If it's one guy. He uses the best

method he has at the time and when it fails he moves to the best one available the next time."

"It's possible," she says. "But it's rare. Most killers have a preferred method and stick to it. But if the murder is just the means to an end and he doesn't care how he achieves it . . ."

I nod as if she can see me.

"Could be a small group of zealots," she says. "Radicalized right-wing nuts who want to silence Malia, enemies of the movement for equality and justice who're taking turns trying to take her out. One guy prefers a gun, one a knife, and one a truck—and a woman in the group prefers to poison. They could even be doing it as a kind of competition—see who gets her first. She's been lucky so far, but that luck's gonna run out eventually."

"I was hoping Merrill or I would be there when it did to stop it from happening," I say.

"Yeah, I'd say her odds of surviving plummeted precipitously when she fired y'all."

s soon as Sam hangs up, I call Tana.

"*John*?" she says in surprise.

"I need to see you," I say. "It's urgent."

"I don't know," she says. "Have you spoken to Malia?"

"You know she won't talk to me," I say. "But it's you I need to see anyway."

"I don't wish you any ill will," she says, as though she should. "I looked into your case and feel bad for what happened. I think you're a good guy, and I don't think you or Merrill would intentionally hurt Malia, but . . . you had to know that when it came out it would do real damage to her and the cause. Edwards has weaponized it against her. It's unbelievable how fast it went viral."

"I'm truly sorry about that," I say. "I thought she knew

and I just didn't think it was something that could be used against her. It's nothing like what she's fighting against."

"Well . . ."

"It's not," I say. "You said you read about what happened. If you did then you'd know it's not."

"I'm not saying it is," she says. "But I am saying it's still a cop killing an innocent civilian—a very young one at that."

I don't say anything. I can't at the moment.

"Sorry," she says. "I'm just saying I think you and Merrill either knew or should have known how it could be used against her."

"I'm very sorry that we didn't," I say. "But we honestly didn't."

"Okay. I believe you."

"I'm still trying to save your boss," I say. "I need your help to do it."

"I just don't think I can. I'm sorry."

"I need you to trust me," I say. "And not in a small way. It's truly a matter of life and death."

"I'm . . ." she says. "My allegiance is to Malia. It feels like a betrayal just to be talking to you like this."

"It's Malia I'm trying to save," I say.

"I don't know . . ."

"Y'all are in real danger," I say.

"I think you should be talking to Malia," she says. "I'm . . . I leave in two days anyway."

"I'm not convinced either of you'll make it until then."

"I'm sorry, John," she says. "I truly am."

38

When Merrill walks into the Holiday Inn hotel lobby the next morning, Rodney is waiting for him.

He's across the way from the PCPD patrol officer assigned to the entryway. When the cop makes eye contact with Merrill, he nods and shoots him with his thumb and forefinger.

"I called because she's not been happy with any of the other security services we've tried," Rodney says when Merrill reaches him. "And I don't think she's safe."

"She ain't," Merrill says as if it's the most obvious statement he's heard in a very long time.

Rodney leads Merrill over toward the elevators.

"I've convinced her to at least consider the possibility

of hiring you back," he says. "But it's not going to be easy."

"Didn't think you were a fan," Merrill says.

"You grew on me," he says as he presses the elevator button. "You do excellent work. And that's what matters most. If something happens to her I want to be able to say I did all I could. Won't be able to live with myself otherwise."

"And we can't have that, can we?" Merrill says.

"Guess I ain't grown on you the way you have me," Rodney says.

The elevator arrives and unloads. Merrill and Rodney step in alone. Rodney presses the button and the doors close.

"You ain't been around much to give it a chance," Merrill says. "Where you been hidin'? Whatcha been doin' with yourself, Rodney?"

"This and that," he says. "Trying to have at least a little bit of a life. If I burn out I won't be good to anyone—especially Malia."

When the elevator stops at the second floor and the doors open, Rodney steps off.

"Malia said you told her we needed to move so we changed rooms."

He had actually suggested that she change hotels, but this is better than nothing.

Reaching Malia's room, Rodney knocks on the door and in a few moments Malia opens it.

"Merrill," she says, as he and Rodney enter the room.

"Malia."

"It's good of you to come," she says. "Especially given the way I spoke to you the last time we were together."

He nods.

"It was an unfortunate situation," she says. "But I wish I would've handled it better."

She waits but Merrill doesn't say anything.

"I was wanting to wait for Tana to join us, but let's go ahead and start. We'll catch her up on everything when she gets here. I'd like to hire you back."

Again he waits, not saying anything.

"I'd want you to be a little more in the background and obviously it'd have to be just you, not John, but if you're willing to come back I'd feel a lot safer. Tana is leaving and I'm going to have to train a new assistant and I'd like to not have to worry about my safety while I do."

"I'd need John in order to be able to do it," Merrill says.

"That's nonnegotiable," she says.

"Just here in the hotel at night and investigating in the background," he says. "Not in public. No one would see him."

She shakes her head. "It's not that I mind. We've looked into his case and sympathize with him. We really do. But Jerry Edwards and others would use it against me. I'm sorry, but I just can't."

Merrill nods and thinks about it.

"Rodney, would you go and see what's keeping Tana?" she says.

"I've tried calling her," he says. "Her room and her cell. She's not answering."

Merrill looks up. "Which room is hers? Do either of you have a key?"

"It's across the hallway and down a few doors," Rodney says, "but we don't have a key."

"Come on," Merrill says.

39

The three of them rush out into the hallway, over to Tana's room, and begin banging on her door and yelling for her.

When there is no response, Rodney says, "I'll go get a key."

Merrill shakes his head. "Not waiting that long. Back up."

Malia and Rodney take a step back and Merrill begins kicking the door, each kick a violent, forceful blow.

As he does, the PCPD cop stationed down by the elevator begins running their way.

On the fifth such kick, concentrated near the handle, the door rips open, slinging into and bouncing off the inside wall behind it.

They can tell immediately that something is wrong.

Merrill runs in first, followed closely by Malia. Rodney, who seems in no hurry to enter the room, brings up the rear in a distant third.

"Oh my God," Malia says, her hand flying up to her mouth. "No. No. No. Please God no."

Tana lies dead on one bed, piles of mail in the process of being sorted on the other, a spilled box of macaroons litters the floor between them, its lid partially propped up on the base of the bedside table.

Her head is cocked in an odd position and her mouth is ringed with what appears to be traces of blood-laced vomit.

Though it's obvious she's dead, both Merrill and Malia reach down and touch her for confirmation.

With her worst fears confirmed, Malia breaks down and begins to sob. "That's supposed to be me," she says. "That was meant for me. She died for me."

"Why the fuck didn't she listen to John?" Merrill says. "*Goddamnit.*"

The uniform appears at the doorway, his gun drawn, his head tilted as he speaks into the radio mic on his shoulder.

"Take her back to her room," Merrill says to Rodney. "I'll take care of this. Don't leave the room. Don't open the door for anyone but me. I'll come over as soon as I can, but it'll be a while."

The cop is already radioing it in, asking for an ambulance, Crime Scene, and a detective.

As soon as Malia and Rodney are gone, Merrill steps over to the cop and tells him the name of the investigator John told him to call if anything happened.

The cop nods and does so without questioning why.

40

For the next few days, as PCPD investigates what exactly happened and who is responsible, Malia mourns for Tana, canceling her events and refusing to come out of her room.

The young detective, a redhead named Pelt and a friend of John Jordan's, seems to be giving Tana's investigation top priority, but doesn't appear to be making much headway in finding out who killed her.

John has visited the hotel twice, expressing his sadness and guilt and regret and requesting to continue to help with the investigation.

"It should've been me," Malia keeps saying. "That poison was meant for me. Not her. Why didn't I think he might try something like that? Why did I let her . . . I should've died instead of that innocent, young woman with her whole life in front of her. My life ended when Graham and Malik died. Why couldn't it have been me?"

At Tana's family's request, there is no public mention of her death—no statement from Malia, no press release, nothing. Later, after they have had sufficient time and privacy to bury and grieve the loss of their daughter, they have agreed to let Malia hold a memorial service in her honor. John, Merrill, and the PCPD believe this could possibly aid the investigation, but Malia doesn't like it.

"That's part of what's so frustrating," Malia is saying. "That I can't do anything for her. There's so much I want to do for that poor sweet girl. And I can't."

"That's not true," Rodney says.

He has come to Malia's room to try one more time to convince her not to cancel her involvement with the upcoming march and rally. He has brought Merrill, who had been sitting outside her door with him.

"There's so much you can do for her," Rodney continues. "And you can do it in honor of her, in her memory. I truly believe that Detective Pelt is going to find the killer. While he's doing that you've got to carry on—for her. Don't quit. Don't let the bastard who did this win. Stop hiding out in here and get back to work—the work that Tana was such a vital part of. If you don't, her death is in vain."

"Don't you dare say that," she says. "No. Her death isn't in vain. No matter what."

"I didn't mean it like that," he says. "I didn't mean it literally. I just meant she would want you to keep doing the work. She wouldn't want you to let the enemies of justice win. Tell her, Merrill."

"You gotta do what you able to," he says. "When you able to. But whatever and whenever . . . don't let the motherfucker who did this make you stop."

She nods very slowly.

"I'll protect you," he says. "You have my word."

"I know you'll do everything you can."

"*Everything* would be to let John find out who did this," he says. "He goin' to anyway. Just be a lot easier you let him do it officially—with your blessing. He's good. The best. Hell, he even warned Tana not to eat any of the stuff that comes in and not to pass any of it along to you."

"He did? Why would she then? I don't understand why she would take a risk like that after she had been warned."

"She probably figured it was okay," he says. "The box of chocolates probably looked sealed and unopened. 'Course, she coulda seen John as disgraced and lacking credibility—just trying to find a way back in. That's what he seems to think—that or that they were actually *from* him."

"That's partly my fault," she says. "The way I spoke to him after the stunt Edwards pulled. The way I fired y'all. I'm sure she thought . . . John must feel . . . awful."

"And then some," Merrill says. "He's already feeling guilty as fuck and now this. I ain't sure he gonna recover."

"I feel so bad for him," she says. "I . . . just can't believe any of this is happening. It hasn't sunk in yet that Tana is really gone. As bad as I feel for John, I can't feel much of anything right now."

"Understandable," Merrill says. "John don't need you to feel bad for him. He needs to work and solve this case. That'd be the best thing for him *and* you."

"Tell him he's got my full support and that I'll do anything I can to help him, but I can't hire him. He can't work for me. I wish he could, but . . . it's just not possible. If he did—in any way—this would all be over and Tana's death would have been in vain."

Merrill starts to say something but Malia's eyes grow wide and she has the look of someone who's just received an unexpected bolt of inspiration.

"Ooh," she says. "Charge me more for your services and slip the money to him."

"It's not about the money. John doesn't care about that."

"*I* do. I want him to be compensated for what he's doing. And the truth is I feel guilty for how I behaved and want to do this."

"None of that'll matter when he finds the killer," he says. "And he *will* find the killer."

"Good," she says. "And then what?"

"And then he'll turn the evidence and the person over to the police," he says. "Knows if he turns 'im over to me I'll eighty-six his ass."

"I vote for that," she says. "Hell, the police may be the ones who did it."

41

I'm sitting in Anna's car in the back parking lot of Pepper's, the popular Mexican restaurant adjacent to the Holiday Inn on MLK that Malia is staying in.

Anna's car is a deep blue Mustang GT with plenty of engine, comfortable leather seats, and a great sound system.

Perfect for tailing Rodney.

While waiting for him to come out I think about the case and what I might have missed.

Sam Cooke is playing softly on the car's Shaker sound system, providing the perfect companionship for thinking and tailing.

Not wanting to lose another soul in my care, I'm working hard to figure out what is happening and who is behind it and vigorously testing every theory I come up with—to the extent I can.

The passenger door opens and Kevin Pelt gets in and closes it.

He's a thirty-something redhead with a boyish freckled face.

His sharp investigative mind and his dogged determinism make him a very good detective and PCPD is lucky to have him.

"What's your unemployed ass up to?" he asks.

"Tailing Rodney Livingston," I say.

"You're in the parking lot of Pepper's," he says.

"Yeah?"

"Why the fuck don't you have some damn tacos up in here?"

"We don't eat in Anna's car," I say. "It's not a rule that's a rule."

"Hell, man, I'll lend you an unmarked or a drug bust car so you can at least eat tacos while you're doing this shit," he says. "I mean, what other pleasures do you have in your life right now?"

"You mean beside that of your company?" I say.

He pulls out his phone and taps his way into his pictures. "So," he says, "I had a little chat with this winner today." He shows me a picture of the pale young man who had stared at Malia so intently at her events before disappearing and not attending any others.

"How'd you find him?" I ask.

"With finely honed skills, an unparalleled investigative mind, and the full resources of the Panama City Police Department behind me."

"What's his story?"

"It's a tragedy," he says. "Raised in the system. In and out of foster homes. Never been arrested, never been caught committing any criminal activity but always seems to be crime adjacent. Says he's a big fan of Malia Goodman's. Thinks she's an angel sent from God with a message we need to hear. Creepy little dude. Definitely the kind that would poison and be miles away when the death occurred. We'll keep an eye on him."

"Thanks," I say. "And not just for that, but for everything—all this. I appreciate it."

"Yeah, well . . . Fuck it, I'm going to get some tacos."

He gets out of the car and I return my attention to the hotel across the way.

From the beginning, Rodney has behaved oddly, inexplicably disappearing for long stretches of time, often not being where he's supposed to be.

Though he's never seen this vehicle, I have no idea how paranoid he is—probably depends on what he's up to—so I'm wearing dark shades, a Robicheaux's Bait and Tackle baseball cap, and the salt-and-pepper stubble from not shaving for the past few days.

When he comes out the hotel and gets into his rental,

I back out of my spot at Pepper's and am waiting for him at the exit as he pulls out onto MLK.

He takes a right on MLK and another on 231—with me following a few car lengths behind him.

He leads me downtown where he has an animated conversation with Khyree Todd in the doorway of an office building on Grace Avenue—at the end of which he pulls a wad of cash out of his pocket and hands it to him.

At first Khyree feigns refusal but is quickly and easily convinced to take the money.

Next Rodney drives down Beach Drive toward St. Andrews, pulling into and parking in the empty parking lot of the permanently closed Buccaneer.

I continue on Beach and turn around at the first side street and head back toward him.

To my amazement, Louden Calhoun has pulled next to Rodney and the two men are having a conversation through the open windows of their vehicles.

Passing by the parking lot again, I drive down around the curve where they can't see me and turn around and head back toward them.

I continue to do this because there is nowhere to park on this part of Beach Drive, but am concerned that they will notice the same blue Mustang passing back and forth.

They talk for a while, and eventually Louden leaves first.

When Rodney pulls back out onto Beach heading west toward St. Andrews, I am actually a few car lengths in front of him.

Turning onto the first street I come to, I let him pass then quickly turn around, then with two cars between us start following him again.

Beach Drive on this early May day is beautiful. To the left, the bay is calm and serene beneath a cloudless powder-blue sky. To the right, the large, old homes with their massive glass fronts and magnificent oaks look down over the bay with a kind of historical majesty.

Rodney winds around Beach at a leisurely pace and eventually winds up at a small, old house on 12th Court where a young woman at least half his age meets him at the door and lets him in.

I pull up and park across the street and a few houses away.

And try to figure out what to do.

Should I confront Rodney now, try to catch him in the middle of something and hope he rattles easily enough to come clean, or wait and gather more evidence and take it to Merrill and Malia?

42

"I see you're still employing the kid killers," Jerry Edwards says.

He is in front of the library with the other protesters, trying to balance himself and his sign on his forearm crutches.

Merrill and Malia have just arrived at the library for the event that had to be rescheduled when the protesters blocked the doors the first time.

This time there is heightened security and the protesters are behind a police cordon off to the side, well away from the door.

A couple of TV news crews are set up near the protesters and have recorded what Edwards said and have now turned their cameras toward Malia and are awaiting her response.

She steps over to them, head up, shoulders back, exuding a fierce strength and confidence.

"Jerry, that's low even for you," she says. "The only person I'm employing is Mr. Monroe, and he's never shot a child. Your inaccuracies and ambushes are the childish attempts for attention of a sad, little man with no following of his own. And they're not just pathetic, they're tiresome and waste the time of serious people working to make our nation and the world a better, safer place for everyone."

His face turns fire-ant red, and he begins to shake and labor to breathe.

"But John Jordan—," he says.

"Is a very fine investigator who has never worked for me," she says. "He does, however, help his friend, Mr. Monroe here, on occasion, which he was doing the night of your little faux debate ambush, which once again shows just how desperate and devious and deplorable you really are. You have been discredited on numerous occasions and I will not waste another second responding to your absurd falsehoods and outrageous half-truths."

Edwards opens his mouth, but nothing comes out.

"To the rest of you protesting," she says, "I invite you to join us inside for a civil presentation followed by a respectful discussion. I am not your enemy. I bet you'll find we're for most of the same things, and those places where we do disagree we can do so without having to vilify each other."

With that she turns and walks inside, Merrill at her side.

When she walks into the meeting room, the crowd waiting for her there welcomes her with a standing ovation.

She steps to the front of the room and thanks them.

Merrill takes a position across from her along the right side wall.

"I can't tell you how glad I am to be with you," she says. "I was so sorry we weren't able to have it when it was originally scheduled, but I am thrilled you came back and that we can be together here tonight."

Another round of applause.

"I want to leave lots of time for questions and comments so we can talk about what you really want to most," she says, "so I think I'll just make few brief remarks about Black Lives Matter, then open it up for your questions. Is that okay?"

They indicate that it is. And they do so in a way that seems to suggest just about anything she wants to do is okay by them.

Merrill scans the audience, searching the room for potential threats. As he does, he wonders where Rodney is. He's supposed to be here and is yet again a no-show.

"When I assert that *black lives matter*," Malia says, "I'm

in no way saying that other lives don't. And yet that is
how so many seem to hear it. We proclaim that *black lives
matter* because we believe there is undeniable, objective
evidence that far too often in this country they don't
matter enough. We are saying that, just as in all places
and all times in all of human history, the minority population, like the poor and the vulnerable and the other or
different, are undervalued by the majority. It's nothing
new. And it's certainly not unique to us. What *is* unique is
that we live in an incredible country where woven into
the very fabric is the ideal that all of us are in fact equals.
So we have a rare opportunity here in the US that so
many others haven't had. We have a foundation that
demands equality under the law and we have a truly
diverse population that affords us the opportunity to put
it into actual practice. So when I say that *black lives matter*
and you say back to me that *blue lives matter* or that *all
lives matter*, of course they do, but that is beside the point.
We're not saying *only* black lives matter. We're just
asserting that they do, in fact, matter because it doesn't
always seem so. My question to those who oppose us,
those who feel the need to make counter assertions, is
why are you so threatened by us saying that we matter
too? It's not an either-or proposition. It's not that black
lives matter *or* blue lives matter. Not that black lives
matter *or* all lives matter. *All* lives matter. And since
certain lives aren't treated like they matter as much as

others, we stand up, raise our voices, peacefully protest, and assert that we matter just as much. Not more, no. But not less either. My husband was a cop. My son was a young black man. When I say black lives matter and that my son's life should not have been taken from him, I am not saying that my husband's blue life doesn't matter or that his life should have been taken from him. But we live in such a what-about-me world where too many among us feel threatened when others only want the same equality that they have. Me being equal doesn't lessen your equality. Not in the least. In fact, you can't be equal if I'm not also equal and vice versa. And think about this, if us asserting that we want to be equal threatens you, then it's not equality we're threatening but the inequality that you're trying to hold on to."

43

"Are you fuckin' following me?"

This is how Rodney greets me when he opens the door, even though there's a young boy beside him.

"Oooh, Mama, Granddaddy used a bad word," the little boy, who looks to be seven or eight, says.

"A real bad one," the young woman who had opened the door and welcomed Rodney in when he first arrived says as she comes up behind them.

"Sorry," Rodney says to her, then looking down at the boy, "Sorry."

"Who are you?" the boy says to me.

"I'm John," I say, and hold out my hand.

"Me too," he says, shaking my hand. "'Cept they call me Johnny. My daddy calls me Johnny Be Good."

"This is that detective I was telling you about," Rodney says to the woman. "He's supposed to be finding out who killed Tana and—he ain't supposed to be following me."

"I'm Vivian," she says. "Rodney's daughter."

"Nice to meet you," I say, shaking her hand.

"We just met Rodney," Johnny says. "Didn't we Mama? Didn't even know I had a Granddaddy Rodney, but I do."

"Come on, Johnny Boy," Vivian says. "Let's let Granddaddy talk to Mr. John."

It's obvious he doesn't want to, but he does what his mom says, albeit slowly and under silent protest.

"The hell you doin' here?" he asks when he closes the door behind him.

"Tryin' to find out where you've been disappearing to," I say.

"Well, now you know," he says. "But you could've just asked."

"Figured if you were willing to tell us you would have."

"I hate that you've wasted valuable time on me," he says. "You're not the investigator Merrill says you are if you think I would ever try to do anything to harm Malia or Tana."

"Does Malia know you've been coming to see your daughter and grandson?"

"She doesn't even know they exist," he says. "I only just found them myself. Haven't told anyone yet. Vivian found me online. Told me she lived in Panama City. Said she wanted to meet. Didn't know I had a grandson until I came over here the first time. Fell in love with the little fella right away. Been comin' over to see them as much as I can. I can only visit when Vivian's husband's not here. He's angry at me on her behalf. Says I'm a piece of shit for abandoning her, not doing anything for her all these years. He works odd hours and he shoots pool in a league. She calls when he leaves and I drop everything and come over. Trying to make up for lost time, see 'em as much as I can while we're in town."

I nod and think about it.

"Can't believe you followed me like I'm some kind of . . . deranged killer or something. I'm Malia's biggest supporter. She couldn't do what she's doing if it weren't for me. I'd never do anything to hurt her or . . ." Tears fill his eyes and he sniffles a little. "Still can't believe Tana's . . . gone." He wipes his eyes and shakes his head. "Such a sweet, sweet girl. Anyway . . . you can confirm everything I've told you with Vivian."

"I will," I say. "But I doubt she'll be able to tell me why you met secretly with Khyree Todd and Louden Calhoun."

44

I slip into Books-A-Million and stand in the back of the crowd gathered to hear Malia speak and have their books signed.

The crowd is large and enthusiastic.

Malia and Merrill, who had come here straight from the make-up library event, are standing to the right side of the table that is set up for the signing, waiting as Malia is being introduced by a young woman from her publishing house.

"Thank you all so much for coming today," she is saying. "I'm Kelly Charles and I have the distinct honor of being Malia's editor. It's a huge responsibility because her books are changing the world. I'm here because I personally drove the books down from our warehouse so no one could buy them all or burn them or do anything else to keep you from getting your copy signed by Malia here today."

The crowd cheers enthusiastically at that. But I believe they would have done the same if she had given directions to the restrooms.

"So that's the main reason I'm here, but . . . since I'm here . . . I get to announce that we've just signed a new deal with Malia for her next two books—and you are not only the first fans to hear the news, but I've also brought mockups of the covers for you to see, so you'll be the first to see those as well. Would you like that?"

They indicate that they would like nothing more.

"Malia's next book will be . . ." She lifts a large card stock poster from the table and holds it up.

The cover shows a gun barrel behind which are the blue lights of a police car, and it reads, *Lethal Force: Where policing went wrong and what to do about it* by Malia Good-man, *New York Times* bestselling author of *Shots Fired.*

"Isn't that beautiful?" Kelly asks. "It's a powerful book and will be out very soon. And then about six months after that we have . . ."

She lifts the second poster from the signing table and holds it up.

The cover shows that statue of Lady Justice with a gun to her head and reads, *Justice for All: Why social movements matter now more than ever* by Malia Goodman, *New York Times* bestselling author of *Shots Fired.*

"So get *Shots Fired* here today and get it signed and then be looking for these two new books coming soon. And now . . . the brilliant woman you all came here to see, the social justice champion who needs no introduction . . . Ms. Malia Goodman."

Malia steps up in front of the table, hugs Kelly and thanks everyone for coming.

As she does, Merrill steps over to where I'm standing.

"So Rodney been playin' grandpappy," he whispers. "You believe him?"

I had called Merrill and let him know what I found out this morning.

"About that part of it," I say. "Mostly. Maybe."

Malia is reiterating some of what her editor said, adding that she is dedicating *Lethal Force* to her assistant, Tana Kay.

She doesn't mention that Tana is dead because the family hasn't given her the okay to do so yet, but she tears up when she mentions her name.

"What about his explanations about meeting with Khyree and Louden?" Merrill asks.

"Not sure if I believe them at all."

Rodney had assured me that he had met with the two men on Malia's behalf, that everything he does is for her and her good. He said that he and Louden had worked out a deal, pending Malia's approval, where if she will agree to lesser charges for them—the State's Attorney is a personal friend of his—that they will release a statement in support of her and that his son Boyd will plead guilty to manslaughter. He said he met with Khyree because he seemed to be putting the brakes on his relationship with Malia—not showing up to as many events, not coming around as much—and it was beginning to affect her work. Said he was just asking the man about his intentions and to see what's going on with him. He explained that the wad of cash he tossed at him was a donation to Khyree's church and that he did it as an angry gesture when he said he wasn't really interested in seeing Malia any longer.

"I asked Malia," Merrill says. "She says she didn't know about any of that."

"All we're asking for is a measured and equal response," Malia is saying. "Why is it that unarmed young black men are shot during routine traffic stops while every effort is made *not* to shoot white domestic terrorists? Local, state, and federal law enforcement agencies bend over backwards to negotiate with heavily armed white killers to surrender peacefully so they don't get hurt—even after they've shot and killed someone, or in many cases several someones—and yet an unarmed black kid following a lawful order to show his driver's license is shot and killed. Did y'all read the local paper this morning? An armed white man with mental issues and PTSD robbed a liquor store in Callaway last night. Gun in hand, hostages, threatening to kill everyone— the hostages, the cops, himself—and yet the police involved spent hours patiently and gently and calmly talking the man into relinquishing his weapon, which turned out to be a starter pistol loaded with blanks, and turning himself in. Nearly the entire time they were doing it they had a clear shot, but they didn't take it. They risked the lives of the hostages and their own lives attempting not to shoot an armed suspect robbing a liquor store and taking hostages. An unarmed black man who was just in there to buy some Bourbon wouldn't have lasted as long. Now, I applaud the peaceful resolution to the dangerous situation. I do. I just want that same careful and measured response for all God's children. And I don't think that's too much to ask."

Hearing Malia say this ignites an idea inside me and I think I might just be able to save a life—though I may have to go to jail to do it.

"I think it's time for a little sit-down with ol' Rodney," Merrill is saying.

"You and Malia? You and me? Who?"

"We'll let Malia have a go at him first—with me there to encourage him to be circumspect in his answers, then depending on how that go . . . you and me may need to have a remedial session of our own."

"Cool," I say, "'cause I've got somewhere I need to be."

"Oh yeah? Where's that?"

"Jail."

45

L ater that afternoon, while Merrill and Malia have a little pow wow with Rodney, I go to jail.

I'm at the Bay County Jail, and I'm here to test a theory.

The desk sergeant had assumed I was here in my official capacity as a Gulf County Sheriff's Investigator—an assumption I didn't disabuse him of.

One of the COs escorts Ricky Lee Canton into the interview room and helps him into his seat, but doesn't remove the handcuffs and leg irons before leaving us alone together.

"What's this about?" he says. "I don't know you."

He's a tall, emaciated white man of indistinguishable age with wide, wild eyes and patches of whiskers on his sunken cheeks.

"No, but you know him, don't you?" I say, holding up a picture of Carmen Sykes on my phone.

"How'd you— Whatta you want, man? Sykes is gone. He's supposed to help me take down the government man, but he's gone. All we are is dust in the wind, man."

With that he confirms my suspicion and may just be able to prove my theory.

"He's gone, but he left you a little something behind, didn't he?" I say.

He shakes his head as if trying to silence a hive of bees buzzing around in it.

"He left you the gun you used to hold up the liquor store last night, didn't he?"

"Weren't no liquor store, man," he says. "It's a front for a child sex ring the shadow CIA is operating."

"Where were you when Sykes got shot?" I ask.

"Sitting behind the tree, man, like contemplating our plan and shit. And here comes fuckin' Sykes, man, haulin' ass, some nigger pig chasing his ass. Sykes shootin' at him, the nigger pig shooting back."

Carmen Sykes had indeed had a gun and was in fact shooting at Trevon Fisher, but it was a starter pistol and it was firing blanks, which is why there was no damage, no evidence anyone but Trevon had fired.

"We were gonna kill pigs, man, and take down the fuckin' federal government and make them take these bugs out of our brains, man, but that nigger pig took Sykes out and now they got me. Ain't it the fuckin' way. House never loses. It's all their money you're playin' with anyway."

"When Sykes was shot, did he toss you the gun behind the tree or did it fall out of his hand and you picked it up?"

"God gave me that gun, man—it fell from heaven out of the hand of Saint Carmen—and he gave me a job to do with it and I failed. I failed so fuckin' bad, man."

I'm hoping that Saint Carmen's prints are still on the pistol, but if they're not, the right investigator or attorney can get the truth out of Ricky Lee so that Trevon won't go down for a righteous shoot.

When I finish with Canton, I call Trevon and tell him.

"I knew I wasn't crazy, but I's beginning to have my doubts," he says. "*Blanks*. Ain't that some shit. I wondered why the windows of my cruiser weren't shot out. I's like . . . this guy's gotta be the worse shot ever. Even running and firing back over his shoulder, he should've hit something. *Blanks*. I'll be damned. Thank you, John. Thank you so much. Still don't know why you did it, but . . . just thank you."

"Happy to help."

"It's hard walking around knowing you've killed someone," he says.

"Yes it is."

"Makes it a little easier knowing he was shooting at you."

"Yes it does," I say. "A little."

46

Malia goes missing the next morning.

"How the hell did this happen?" Rodney says. "You promised her you'd protect her. I heard you tell her."

"We'll find her," I say. "We'll get her back."

The three of us are in Malia's hotel room looking around.

I step away from the two of them and call Detective Blake Greeley in Chicago.

"You still got eyes on the two suspects up there?" I ask.

"Been a few days," he says. "I'll check. Any particular reason?"

I tell him.

"*Ho*-ly fuck," he says. "I'll get back to you as soon as I can."

I say, "Thanks," but he's already off the call.

I step back over to Merrill and tell him what Greeley said.

Rodney tries to ask about it, but Merrill shuts him down. "No time now," he says. "We'll tell you later."

"Let's talk through what happened," I say. "Try to figure out who took her."

"Since it's just me now," Merrill says, "we been doin' this thing where once she's in for the night, I go grab a few hours of sleep."

"You were *sleeping* when this happened?" Rodney says, his voice rising in pitch and volume.

"Rodney, I swear to God . . ." Merrill says. "Either go play with your grandkid or shut the fuck up. You say another word and *you'll* be missin'."

"Obviously, you have to sleep," I say. "She made the decision to hire just you back."

"Made her swear to me she wouldn't open the door for anyone—whether she knew them or not. Somebody come to the door, she call me. She need anything, she call me. She can't sleep or has a hangnail, she call me. Last night she said Khyree Todd coming over to talk. Say it won't take long. They breaking up, just tryin' to be adults about it. Say she ain't going out again and she'd give me a call when he left. Sure enough, 'bout half hour later, she call, say he leaving and that she's turning in. She been sleeping a lot more since Tana died. I even looked out through my peephole and watched him leave. Waited a while, made sure he didn't come back. Then I turned in. When I hadn't heard from her by the regular time this morning, I called her. When I got no answer, I banged on her door, then broke it in."

I nod as I try to figure out a few things.

"Called you next," he says. "Know police won't even take a report, let alone do anything. Know you my best chance of finding her anyway."

"How did she seem?" I ask.

"Good," he says. "She was thrilled about Trevon Fisher. Couldn't wait to announce it at the rally. Still sad about Tana. More than sad—distraught. And she frustrated as fuck with this fool—" he jerks his head toward Rodney, "—but in general she was good."

"How long did you wait before making sure Khyree was gone?" I ask.

He shrugs. "Not sure. Felt like a while but it was probably only about five minutes or so. I could've imagined it but I thought I heard the elevator arrive, open, and leave."

"You probably did," I say, "but Khyree is as good a place to start as any. Maybe he waited a while and came back and since he had just been in her room she didn't view him as a threat. She probably thought he forgot something. He may even have in order to get back in."

"Should we split up in case it's not him?" Merrill says. "Who else should we look at?"

"It could be anybody," I say. "Some random psycho or obsessed fan we've never heard of, but if it's not . . . If it's someone we know, I'd say the most likely suspects besides Khyree are Louden Calhoun, Jerry Edwards, and Rodney."

Rodney starts to show his outrage at the suggestion, but Merrill shoots him a particularly wicked look and he refrains.

"Okay, let's start with them," he says. "I'll take Louden and his crew and you take Khyree. I'll take ol' Rot-nee here with me and interrogate his ass on the way. Two birds. One Merrill. We still don't find her, we meet back up and hit up Edwards together."

47

"We had a very cordial breakup," Khyree is saying. "If you can even call it that. I'm not sure we were together enough to need a breakup, but . . . it was nice to talk about things and not have to have any assumptions or misunderstandings. It was the most mature, adult parting of the ways I've ever been a part of."

I have surprised Khyree Todd at his house—a modest starter home in an aging subdivision in Lynn Haven, a small city next to and considered part of Greater Panama City.

He has surprised me by coming to the door in his bathrobe.

"Why do you ask?" he says. "I really never expected to hear anything from Malia or any of you again."

"You're not going to the rally and the march?" I ask.

"Of course, but I'll just be— I didn't mean I wouldn't ever see her again, just that—"

"Who broke up with whom?"

"What? Why? What does it matter? What did she say?"

"I'd like to know how you see it."

"This seems to be going far beyond providing security for her and figuring out who tried to kill her and got poor Tana instead."

"I'll explain in a moment," I say. "You'll understand then. Please just answer my questions as honestly as you can. It's important."

"Mind if I get dressed first?"

"It'll only take another minute. It really is important."

"Sure. Okay. No problem. It really seemed mutual. But maybe I wanted to break up a little more than she did —or wanted to a little sooner. But we agreed it was never a long-term thing. She'll be leaving town in a few days. We always knew that."

"Then why not just wait until then?"

"Well . . . I'm not sure exactly. These things seem to have a life of their own and once you start talking about them . . . they just sort of go where they go."

"Why did you want to stop seeing her?"

"She's a little too old for me," he says. "She's very, very busy and going through so much right now. And our personalities were just . . . a little too different. You know what it's like when you almost spark with someone but you don't quite? It was like that."

"Why did she say she wanted to stop seeing you?"

"She said the thing about us always knowing it was short-term and that she had so much going on and that she was in shock and grief about Tana. She really is. She can't stop crying, just can't get it together for more than a little while at a time. Anyway . . . that sort of thing. I think the worse thing she said the entire time was that I was a distraction—and that's not all that bad, is it?"

"After you left her room the first time, did you go back?"

He shakes his head. "No. Why?"

"Not at any time for any reason?"

"No. I never went back to her room. Not last night. Not today. Why? Why are you asking me all this? Why does any of it matter? She can't be upset by this. She was so—"

"She's missing," I say.

"*What*? Since when? Oh, God. You think I had something to do with it. I didn't, I swear to you. I would never do anything but help her. I have nothing but respect and admiration for her and the work she's doing."

"Where have you been and what have you been doing since you left Malia's room last night?"

"I came straight back here," he says. "Been here ever since. Haven't left."

"Anyone verify that?"

"Ah . . ."

"Mind if I search your house?"

"Well . . ."

"Well what? Do you have a problem with me searching your house?"

"No . . . but . . ."

"What did Rodney want when he came to see you yesterday? What was he paying you for?"

"He asked why I wasn't coming around as much, why I wasn't returning Malia's calls and texts. Asked me not to break up with her just yet. Just to keep seeing her until they left town."

"What'd you tell him?"

"That I would talk to her, but that I couldn't pretend to be interested."

"What'd he pay you for?"

"He didn't pay me for anything. He said, 'Just do what I ask for a few more days. Here's a donation to your church. More where that came from—a lot more—if you'll pretend to be into her until we leave.' And he just tossed it at me and left. I left the money at the front desk for him when I came and talked with Malia."

"Ever left anything else at the front desk? For Malia? Anyone?"

"No. Why?"

"You gonna let me search your house or do I have to call my buddies at the Bay County Sheriff's Department and have them do it?"

"Well . . . the thing is. This is kind of . . . embarrassing. But there's someone here. I don't mind you searching, but . . . I just need to come clean. I just feel so bad, so . . . The real reason I broke up with Malia is . . . my ex-girlfriend and I got back together. That's the . . . Anyway, she's here. You can search, but I feel ashamed and embarrassed. We just . . . We hadn't finished what we had and when she called . . ."

"How long she been here?"

He looks sheepish. "Since last night."

"No. Exactly what time did she arrive?" I ask, then looking around add, "Where is her car?"

He looks even more sheepish now. "She came with me. She . . . well . . . she was actually waiting in the car while I went in and had my talk with Malia."

"Then instead of ashamed or embarrassed you should be grateful."

"Why's that?"

"Because you have an alibi."

48

Merrill and Rodney meet Louden Calhoun in the same spot in the parking lot of the Buccaneer that Rodney had met him in the day before.

Part of Rodney proving to Merrill that he wasn't involved in Malia's disappearance was to get Louden to meet them, which he did willingly.

When the darkly tinted window rolls down and it's Merrill, Louden looks surprised but recovers quickly.

"What is this?"

"A test," Merrill says. "What did you and Rot-nee here talk about when you met yesterday?"

Louden looks over at Rodney.

"Don't look at him," Merrill says. "Look at me. Tell the truth as if your life depends on it."

Louden looks from Merrill's arm down to the car door. "Do you have a gun pointed at me?"

"Probably can't ever go wrong assuming I do."

"Goddamn, I wish I'd've never gotten mixed up with y'all."

"Feeling is mutual. Only more so. So what'd y'all talk about?"

"Are y'all not on the same side or something?" Louden asks.

"Just answer the question. Tell the truth and you have nothing to worry about. I'm on the side of truth. Are you on our side?"

Louden tells him essentially the same story Rodney had.

"And that's it?" Merrill asks.

"That's it."

"You or any of your band of idiots had any other contact with Malia or anyone else from her organization?"

"No, and don't want any. We just want this to be over. I want my boy back. He's a good kid. A good cop. He made a mistake. A horrible mistake. There was nothing malicious behind it. No ill intent. Just a terrible mistake. I don't want him to be a martyr to some cause, a scapegoat for those demanding blue blood. That's all. I've always been honest about that. Y'all helped that black cop, why not Boyd? I've been stupid. I admit it. I let some young fools talk me into some truly boneheaded actions, but . . . that's all I'm guilty of. I swear. What's this about? Can we do this deal or not? Please. My son will be punished. I just don't want him to lose the rest of his life."

"Like the unarmed kid he shot in his grandmother's backyard?" Merrill says.

"We're done here," Louden says, and cranks his vehicle. "We came to y'all with a simple, reasonable deal. We'll take our chances with the jury. Hell, maybe they'll come back before the rally."

"Y'all trying to delay the rally, that it?" Merrill asks.

"Huh? How? Tell me how we could do that. I've told you what we're trying to do. Make a reasonable deal so my son doesn't lose his entire life."

"Malia's missing," Merrill says, and watches closely for Louden's reaction.

"What? When? You think somebody took her? You think we took her? No way. No fuckin' way. We're already out on bail waiting for our hearing for the other stupid shit we did. I would never kidnap anyone for any reason. Not ever."

"Not even to save your son?"

"Not even if it would, but taking her wouldn't do that. Wouldn't stop the jury verdict or even the rally. And it would focus far more attention on her and her cause. We'd be the first to be suspected. I swear to you—on the life of my son—we did not take her and have absolutely nothing to do with who did."

Merrill is inclined to believe him.

"How did it happen?" Louden asks. "When?"

Merrill tells him.

"Was the door broken down?"

Merrill shakes his head.

"Then you have to know it wasn't us. She would never open the door for us."

"Had that thought myself," Merrill says.

"Then why all—"

"Have to be sure," Merrill says. "You could've had another cop buddy of yours flash a badge and get in."

"A cop is the last person she would let in. She would've called you no matter who it was, but especially a cop."

"Probably so."

"We didn't take her," Louden says, "but by God we can help you find her. We'll do all we can—whether y'all help Boyd and us with our legal situations or not. We'll help you find her. Let me put out some feelers. I'll be in touch."

49

"So that leaves us with Jerry Edwards," Merrill is saying.

I nod. "Unless one of Greeley's guys is down here. Still haven't heard back from him."

We are in the lobby of the Holiday Inn trying to figure out our next move.

"Could be them," Merrill says. "Could be anybody—including ol' albino boy who vanished on us, but my money's on Edwards."

"I'll give Greeley a call to see if he's found out anything yet," I say.

I step away from them toward the seating area to the right where I first met with Tana and call Greeley.

"Was just about to call you," he says. "Got eyes on my guy. He's still here. But the Aryan Brotherhood prick got bonded out and we've lost track of him. I'm working on finding him now. I'll let you know as soon as I know something. But, *fuck*, if I was wrong about him and he's got her..."

I thank him and walk back over to Merrill and Rodney.

"We have any idea where Edwards is staying—if he's even still in town?" Merrill asks.

"I've made some calls," I say. "Nothing so far. We need to all use every contact we have."

"Louden Calhoun just offered his help," he says. "Why don't you give him a call, Rodney? See if they can help us locate him."

Rodney walks about ten feet away and makes the call.

"I'll put a few feelers out," Merrill says, "but you know ... I bet ol' Trevon Fisher and PCPD feelin' awful grateful to your ass about now."

"I'll reach out," I say.

"Cool."

"If it *is* him," I say, "and he plans to take her back to Chicago ... he won't have gotten very far yet."

"That'd be best case scenario," he says. "More afraid what he might have already done to her."

"I think there's three most likely scenarios," I say. "He's obsessed with her and in some twisted way wants to be a couple."

"Really?"

I nod. "He's definitely obsessed. And usually when it's to that degree there's a sexual component."

"Oh fuck."

"Another possible scenario is that he just wants to harm or kill her," I say. "But if so, why take her? Why not just do it there?"

"That what he been trying to do all along," Merrill says. "Makes sense he'd do it when he had the chance and get the hell away."

"If it's the harm or kill her scenario," I say, "the only reasons I can see for him taking her is because he thought he might get caught before he could finish or that he wanted to take his time and torture her."

"Fuck," Merrill says. "Just keeps getting worse and worse."

"The third and best scenario is that he just kidnapped her to prevent her from attending the rally tomorrow and is just holding her somewhere and will let her go after it's over."

"Hell, I hope it's that," he says. "But I'm tellin' you, she really embarrassed him in front of the library. The news cameras were rolling and it got reported. You could see him just seething. I have a hard time believing it's the third scenario."

I nod. "You're probably right. It'll just depend on how deranged he really is. I'll be shocked if he's not secretly sexually obsessed with her and that's his motivation behind everything."

"I just can't even picture his broken down ass being sexual," he says.

"Doesn't have to be physical to be sexual," I say. "And sometimes the most sexually motivated are the least physically capable of sex. Leaves everything in the realm of frustration and fantasy."

"Like when these sick fucks use knives 'cause they can't use their little dicks?"

I nod. "Of course, there's a fourth scenario," I say.

"*Fuck*," he says, his voice full of drama and exaggeration.

"It could not be him at all," I say. "We could be wasting our time looking for him when someone else altogether has her."

50

By late that night we have exhausted all our contacts and are out of options.

I feel frustrated and useless.

I am increasingly apprehensive.

What am I not seeing? Where did I go wrong? Who has her? If Edwards, where does he have her?

Because of her public profile and the threats and attempts on her life she has received, law enforcement agencies have gotten involved sooner than they normally would. In addition to releasing a BOLO on both Malia and Edwards, they're actually already doing some investigating into her disappearance.

"What we do now?" Merrill asks.

I frown, shake my head, and shrug. "I honestly don't know. I'm at a loss."

Rodney has retired to his room. Merrill and I are in ours sitting in the two seats next to the window, watching the traffic on MLK.

"Cops better equipped to deal with searches like this than us," he says.

I nod. "True."

"But?"

"But . . . they are working on multiple missing persons, have several other cases and concerns and distractions and . . . aren't personally invested in this one. Chances are . . . if they find Edwards or Malia at all it will be because they happen upon them."

He nods and frowns.

"And every minute that passes, the likelihood of finding her alive decreases significantly."

"Rodney was right," he says. "This is my fault."

I shake my head. "No way. Absolutely not. It was an impossible situation. You did everything you could."

"Not everything."

"Her room wasn't broken into," I say. "She had to let them in for some reason—and she did so without calling you."

"He coulda got a keycard to her room."

"Still couldn't get in if she had the deadbolt engaged."

"*Fuck*," he says.

"I know."

"So what's our next move?"

"Don't think we have one until the rally tomorrow," I say. "Edwards is supposed to be at it live broadcasting his radio show. If he's not there, we have to figure it's him and keep looking for him. If he is there, we follow him and hope he leads us to her."

51

The Rally for Peace and Justice takes place in McKenzie Park following the March for Equality that emanated from an African Methodist Episcopal church on MLK and ended at the park.

A large crowd of marchers had slowly walked down the middle of the street singing "We Shall Overcome" and chanting various slogans about peace and equality, as counter protesters, many of them with Confederate and Nazi flags, lined the sidewalks hurling insults and shouting slogans of their own.

Beneath the tall, ancient, spreading oaks of McKenzie Park, a lively and engaged crowd is gathered. The focus is on the permanent covered pavilion stage on the far side of the park. Songs are sung. Speeches are given. Banners and signs are waved.

Lining the left side of the park a row of popup tents houses food and art vendors, while on the right side media outlets covering the event are set up and broadcasting, the bright logos of their vans framed prominently behind them.

A not insubstantial police presence is posted around the perimeter. Beyond them on the fringe of the park and of life, White Nationalists, members of the KKK, and various other rightwing racist groups hold flags and signs of their own, but mostly hold their tongues.

Those gathered nearly quadruples those who participated in the march.

The speakers, which include Khyree Todd, are good, by turns inspiring and profound, but there's a sense that everyone is waiting for Malia, wondering where she is, why she didn't participate in the march.

Rodney is on the stage, introducing speakers and keeping the program going. Merrill and I are in the back not far from the big fountain on Harrison.

"Look who showed up to broadcast his hate," Merrill says.

I follow his gaze over to see Jerry Edwards inside a tent booth with his name on it in amongst the legitimate news organizations.

"I can't decide if I feel more relief or dread at seeing him here," I say.

"Think it means he doesn't have her?"

"Probably," I say. "Or that he doesn't have her anymore."

"If he killed that amazing woman . . ." he says, letting the obvious implications hang out there like the vow they are.

We are quiet a moment, still scanning the crowd and stage.

I text Greeley to see if he's found the Aryan Brotherhood suspect yet.

He texts back almost immediately to say they still haven't located him.

"You need to say how we gonna do this," Merrill says, "'cause if it's up to me I'm just gonna go start pummeling his ass."

And then I notice something.

"Look over there again," I say. "Not just at him but at all media outlets."

He does.

"Notice anything?" I ask.

"He the only one without a van behind him."

"And we know he has one because we saw it at the library and the debate at the Martin and at Books-A-Million."

"Let's go find it."

We rush out of the park and over to the right side where the media is set up. Going behind the line of vans and satellite trucks, we search for Edward's van, but are unable to find it in among the myriad vehicles jammed in the area.

"You'd think with as many fuckin' marchers as there were, they'd be less cars 'round here," Merrill says.

Across the side street from the park I see the full parking lot of the old Fiesta, and think of Angel Diaz, Acqwon Lewis, and their group of high school friends who spent a magical night downtown that included dancing and drinking at the Fiesta and ended with the disappearance of Angel and the arrest of Acqwon.

At the far end of the Fiesta parking lot along Beach Drive I see Jerry Edwards's van.

"There it is," I say.

"Let's go," he says, and takes off running.

I join him and say, "We should call PCPD and have them get a search warrant so he can be prosecuted if we find . . . something."

"Never thought I'd say this to you, but you sound like a fuckin' cop."

"Well, I sort of still am," I say. "And I don't want Edwards walking because I did a search of his property without a warrant."

"You not doin' a search of his property," he says. "I am. And I'm just a private citizen. It's just a little B and E for me. By the time you come along the van will be open and you'll be able to see inside and if there's anything to see you'll have your probable cause."

"You better run faster, you gonna do all that before I get there," I say.

He speeds up but so do I.

I'm not going to play procedural games with Malia's life on the line. If Edwards took her I want him to go to prison for it, but right now I want to find Malia more. And as quickly as possible.

When we reach the panel van with the huge pictures of Edwards's face on each side, we look through the windows in the front but can't see into the back.

We try both doors but find them locked.

Rushing around to the back doors, we try them. They're also locked.

Merrill runs back up to the front driver's side.

I follow him.

When he reaches the front driver's side door, he withdraws his .45 and begins to bang on the glass with the butt of it.

After several hard whacks it finally breaks and he is able to reach in and unlock all the doors as the alarm starts to sound.

We run to the back of the van and fling open the doors.

52

The back of the van is mostly empty.

Some clothes, books, mics, cables and other broadcasting equipment, but no Malia. No sign she had ever been back here.

"Come on," Merrill says. "Alarm's gonna attract attention."

He takes off up Beach Drive, beside the old Fiesta building and right on Harrison to circle back around to the park.

By the fountain next to the old Sherman Arcade building, we take a right and leisurely walk back into the park, making sure the base of a thick-bodied oak blocks us from Edwards's view.

He looks around suspiciously, eventually craning his neck around behind him toward his van. Seeing the lights flashing, he removes his headphones and places his microphone down. Limping out of his booth and out into the side street, he points his fob toward his van, pressing the button to silence the alarm.

He doesn't walk all the way over to the van, just pauses there a moment then starts back.

"Have you ever seen anyone do a live radio broadcast without a crew?" I ask. "Every other time we've seen him he's had staff with him."

Merrill nods. "Wonder what his ass up to that he wants to be alone?"

I pull out my phone and find Edwards's website where his live broadcast is streaming. When I tap on the Listen Live link, Edwards's in-progress commentary of the rally starts playing.

"How he do that?" Merrill says. "Bitch can throw his voice like a mofo, can't he?"

"I'm thinking this is a clue," I say.

When Edwards comes back, he scans the crowd with a rueful smile on his face as he puts on his headphones and picks up his mic and starts talking into it again.

"Who the hell he talkin' to?" Merrill says.

"That's what I'm wondering."

For all his looking around and constantly scanning the crowd, Edwards continually glances at one spot in particular.

"He always comes back to that same spot," I say,

turning to look in that direction. "It's odd too. It's up high and out of the park."

When I see the spot he's been looking at, I know where Malia is.

"Look over there," I say. "He keeps glancing back at that window in the top of the Sherman Arcade. I bet he's got her tied up in there so she can see the rally going on without her."

Before I've even finished what I'm saying, I'm moving in that direction, Merrill right beside me.

We run over to the building, into the open breezeway and up the stairs to the apartments in the back that over-look the park.

As we approach the door we can hear someone talk-ing, so instead of busting it down, we knock.

When there is no answer after several knocks, we bust it down.

Inside, Malia is bound standing to a hand truck, near the window in the back. From a speaker near her, Edwards is taunting her.

"Motherfucker is broadcasting just to her," Merrill says.

Technically it's narrow casting—very narrow casting —but I don't mention it.

As Merrill unties her, I ask, "Are you okay?"

"I will be," she says. "Just get me to that stage."

53

A s we get Malia cleaned and ready she quickly tells us about her ordeal.

Because he had just left, she opened her hotel door for who she thought was Khyree who had either forgotten something or had changed his mind about them breaking up. But it was Edwards.

He was on her so fast, his hand covering her mouth, the weight of his body pressing down on her, that she didn't have time to scream. She quickly discovered that he's not injured or feeble, but agile and strong.

He brought her here to this Air B&B apartment he is staying in while in town, and has alternated between acting like they're a couple who will live happily ever after to degrading and taunting her like a captor in a prison war camp.

And though he has touched and kissed and groped her, he has not raped her—but she had little doubt that that's what he was working up to.

But the thing that gave him the greatest pleasure of all was keeping her from speaking at the rally, and making her watch it while hearing his thoughts and commentary about it.

"He's deranged and dangerous," she says. "Be careful with him."

"Oh, I'm gonna be real careful with his evil ass," Merrill says.

While I escort Malia to the stage, Merrill makes his way over to Edwards's booth, and though I am unable to see the altercation, when we reach the stage Merrill is holding Edwards in a chokehold, his arms behind him, his right eye swollen, his nose bleeding.

As soon as Malia steps on the stage the crowd erupts in applause and cheers.

When they have settled down, which takes a few moments, she explains why she is just arriving at the rally.

"I'm so sorry I missed the march and that I'm just getting here for the rally, but I wouldn't be here at all if it weren't for Merrill Monroe Security and Investigations. Last night I was kidnapped out of my hotel room by Jerry Edwards. He has held me hostage from then until just a few moments ago when Mr. Monroe and his associates freed me. Mr. Monroe has apprehended Mr. Edwards and is detaining him until the police, who are on their way, arrive. Jerry Edwards, like so many others, tried to stop the progress of equality and justice and peace, but he, like they, failed. And they will keep on failing as long as we stick together in taking a stand for what is right and good and just."

As Malia goes on to deliver a resplendent and rousing speech—perhaps the best of her life—PCPD arrives, takes Jerry Edwards into custody and begins the investigation, and it's difficult to imagine a more dramatic backdrop for the off-the-cuff, heart-felt comments Malia is making.

54

"I figured out who sent you the threatening postcards and made the attempts on your life," I say.

"Jerry Edwards, right?" Malia asks.

We are in her hotel room. It's later that night and the first chance we've had to talk. It's just the two of us. Merrill is being interviewed by PCPD and Rodney is at his daughter's house. Both will be back soon.

I shake my head.

"It's also the same person who killed Tana," I say.

"Jerry didn't do that either?" she asks.

I shake my head again.

"Then who?"

"You," I say.

The moment the word comes out of my mouth she breaks down and begins to sob.

I had expected protests and denials, but she looks genuinely relieved to be caught.

She cries long and hard, her body heaving in guilt and grief.

I'm meeting with her alone in an attempt to save her from the dark abyss she is so precariously teetering over.

It's extremely encouraging that she's not denying it.

"*Oh, God . . .*" she says.

Her words are coming through gasps and violent wretches of bitterness and regret.

I wait.

The dim hotel room is perfectly still and completely silent—apart from Malia's moans and movements.

"I'm . . . so . . . sorry. I can't believe I . . . Poor Tana. *Oh . . . God.*"

I continue to wait as she continues to mourn both her own depravity and the death of her closest companion.

In addition to denials I expected eventual justifications and rationalizations. She's offering neither—only remorse and regret, sadness and pain, guilt and grief.

Eventually, between gasping heaves she says, "How . . . did . . . you . . . know?"

"I've been suspicious for a while," I say. "The near-miss attempts on your life—so many of them and they didn't quite add up. Every one of them were ones that could be done alone and there were no witnesses. The only exception to that was the drive-by in Atlanta, which

really was a random thing y'all happened to be close to—
which is why the threatening postcard you sent for it was
after the fact. And it was too easy for you to pick up
vintage postcards in the towns you were in and slip them
into your own mail when no one was looking. But the
other two attempts—they were just you alone. You could
easily fake someone breaking into your hotel room—
someone that had to be very athletic and acrobatic just to
get in, and then when he does, he doesn't know whether
he wants to rape you or kill you and then he does neither
and leaves his knife behind. And the hit and run. From
the beginning I thought the timing of that was impossible
—and not just you leaving the hotel unexpectedly late at
night after faking a phone call to yourself from within the
hotel to drive on your own to your next gig, which meant
only Rodney, Tana, and the organizer of the next gig
knew. By doing it that way you ensured that the eventual
intended victim looked like a suspect. But it wasn't just
the timing of the trip itself. It was the timing of hitting a
traveling car on a dark road from the side. It'd be a challenge for the best of professional drivers. Unless the
vehicle being hit is stopped. The cops up there theorized
there were two people—one to stop you and one to hit
you with the truck. But it was all you. You stole the truck.
You stopped your vehicle. You drove the truck into it.
Even the tracks in the snow confirm this. There was just
one set. And then you drove the truck a little ways down

the road and left it and walked back to play the victim, fake concussion and all. That's why the truck wasn't taken far. You had to walk back."

She nods slowly.

"The concussion *was* fake, right?" I ask.

"I hit the window with my jack then pretended to have a concussion. They sent me to the hospital to get checked out and I was able to convince the emergency room attending."

A door down the hallway bangs shut and the muffled sounds of kids running seep through the walls and invade the quiet of the room.

"You've had genuine threats against you, like the caller to the college radio station who said you were going to leave Panama City in a body bag, which made it more difficult to see that you were the one doing these."

"The real threats were what gave me the idea to even do it," she says.

"But it wasn't until I realized that your dyslexia is so severe that effectively you can't read or write and that Tana was writing your books and your speeches that I began to really see. I saw just how valuable she was to you, just how embarrassed you were about your disability, just how desperate you were to keep her. She was so loyal, so devoted to you—and to the movement—that she was thrilled just to have a small co-writing credit on your new book that she wrote. And she was hoping that would launch her into her own career—to actually get credit for the books she writes."

She shakes her head. "Poor thing. I . . ."

She is overcome with emotion again.

"Two things I've been wondering," I say. "The first is . . . given the severity of your dyslexia . . . How did you write the postcards? Did you use some sort of talk-to-text app or program?"

She nods. "Yeah. Took me a while to figure it all out—especially lining up the postcards in the printer—went through a lot of postcards experimenting, but finally was able to speak the note into my phone, email it to myself, and print the postcards from my computer."

"The second is . . . how did you get the same partial print to be in both Chicago and Madison? That was a very, very nice touch. The only thing I could come up with was that you stole the knife from the truck or from the place where you stole the truck."

She nods again. "That's exactly what I did," she says. "I had no idea they'd just find partial prints. I just wanted to link the two crimes. Figured if a knife from the truck was used they'd think the same person did both—even if the prints belonged to the truck owner and they could rule him out. I guess the prints got smudged enough to be partial. I don't know. That part wasn't planned."

Unlike her previous room this one isn't as bright and doesn't smell as pleasant. It's a little dingy and smells like a place where many people have passed through—the lingering odors of sweaty feet and dirty socks, unwashed hair and sleep and the hint of cigarette smoke all hovering just beneath the unnatural aroma of commercial cleaning products.

"The entire time I was hoping I wasn't right," I say. "I have such respect for you, so appreciate what you're doing and the way you're doing it. I figured when only the chocolates with coconut in them—the ones Tana always took for herself because you don't eat coconut—were poisoned it had to be you, but I didn't know for sure until the event at Books-A-Million when your editor revealed your new book covers that it was you. Not only did you not give Tana a co-writing credit on the book you supposedly wrote together, but you stole her book that she had given you to blurb. She had told me her book was about social movements, and sure enough after she dies your new book is about social movements."

She keeps shaking her head, seemingly unable to comprehend what she's done.

"She . . . Do you know . . . what she did?" she asks. "She . . . actually made me a recording of her reading the entire book out loud, knowing . . . I couldn't really read it otherwise. How could I have . . . done what I did . . . to her . . . of all people?"

I nod. "That is the question," I say. "And you're not the first to ask it."

"You . . . you probably won't . . . believe me, but . . . I started the threatening postcards and fake attempts on my life . . . not . . . to set up . . . killing her . . . but to . . . try to get her to stay with me."

"I actually do believe that," I say. "I believe you're a good person, maybe even a great one, who has done some truly remarkable things, and that you got caught up in—"

"It wasn't until I read her book—well, listened to it— and realized how good it was and how I'd never have another one come out and everyone who read hers would know she had been the one writing mine all along that I decided to . . ."

"Kill her?" I offer.

"I can't even say it," she says. "I told myself I was . . . trying to save the movement, that it wouldn't go on . . . without me."

I think about the way the actions of Jerry Edwards and Malia Goodman mirror each other, and how many leaders of movements, zealots of causes, rigidly righteous people are capable of justifying some of the most atrocious and inhumane behavior.

"I'm sure part of you really believed that. And I think it's partly true. It will go on, but—"

"But the damage I have done to it," she says. "I welcome punishment. I deserve it. You . . . can't imagine how glad I am you caught me. Truly. I still can't believe I actually did it—that I . . . was capable of it. I . . . wish . . . I wish they'd give me the electric chair for it. I truly do. But, *God*, I hate what this is going to do to the work."

"I know."

We are quiet for a long, dark time.

"Why did you hire Merrill?" I ask.

"Because of the genuine threats," she says. "And Rodney and Tana kept pushing me to hire security. I thought it'd look suspicious if I didn't. But I had no idea he planned on bringing an investigator with him. I thought I was just getting security, which I needed."

I nod slowly and think through what she has said.

"I still can't believe I really did it," she says again. "Part of me still doesn't think I did, thinks there's no way I'm capable of something like that."

"Would you take it back if you could?"

"Are you kidding?" she says. "I'd give anything to take it back. Anything."

"Your own life?"

"Gladly. I wish I had never been born instead of doing something like this. I killed another human being—a good, smart, kind, faithful, loving, innocent person. God, what I wouldn't give to trade places with her right now."

"I can't tell you how many killers I've heard say that over the years," I say. "You'd be surprised, but nearly all but a very few would take it back if they could."

"I don't doubt it," she says. "It's truly like another person did it. Like it wasn't me. I don't recognize that person. I don't want to be that person, to ever have been her."

"And every time, every single time a killer says to me they wish they could take it back I feel so powerless, so helpless to help them, because what can I do? I can't bring their victims back from the dead. I can't undo what they have done. Just once I wish I could, that I could reverse time somehow or go back far enough to prevent it. But I can't. Maybe if I had been able to see it before it happened. Maybe if I could have suspected a little sooner, somehow predicted what a murderer might do, but . . ."

She nods. "I'd give anything if—"

"If this time I could have seen the possibility of the murder before it was committed? But what if I actually needed it committed to test my theory, to make sure I was right? I'd have to . . . gather up all the chocolates. I'd have to go to all the local stores to see if they could have been purchased in close proximity to the hotel where the would-be killer was staying. I'd have to have a friend at FDLE get the lab to test it. And even if I was able to do all that . . . I'd still have to convince the would-be victim to trust me enough to let me administer a neurotoxin that mimics death, one that drops the heart rate to unbelievably low levels, lowers the breathing to three or four times per minute, and drops the body temperature because the blood flow is so low. And I'd have to have a friend whose girlfriend is a doctor who could administer it to ensure the would-be victim didn't get too much and suffer brain damage. I'd have to convince a detective friend of mine over here to trust me enough to let me try it. I'd have to do all that—possibly after being fired by the would-be murderer. And if I was able to do all that . . . what kind of person would be worth it? What would-be murderer would be valuable enough both in her own right and to a cause or movement that she would be worth doing all that?"

"You're not . . . Are you saying you—"

She stops as we hear a light tap on the door.

"Please," she says, as she jumps up and runs over to the door. "Please. Please. Please be . . ."

She flings open the door without checking the peephole and sees Tana standing there, collapsing to the floor and squalling in what sounds like both agony and ecstasy as she does.

55

S tepping around Malia, Tana walks into the room and stands near me.

The door bangs shut behind her.

There's something markedly different about her—in her posture and bearing, in her piercing and intense eye contact—as if any insecurity and timidity went the way of her naiveté and innocence. There's nothing shrinking or mousy about her. Very little of the woman I first encountered in a room not dissimilar to this one remains in this one.

Eventually, Malia pulls herself together and stands.

The contrast between the two women—between each other, between who they used to be and who they are now—is startling. Tana is empowered, emboldened. Malia is weakened, wounded.

"I can't tell you how glad I am you're alive," she says. "I've never been happier to see someone in my entire life."

"I just knew John had to be wrong," Tana says. "I told him he was insane to think that you would ever want to harm me in any way. And not just because of all I had done for you, how much of my life I had given you, but . . . because there's no way you're the kind of person who would kill another person. There's no possible way. Not a chance."

"Oh, God, Tana, I'm so sorry."

Tana continues. She isn't really talking to Malia as much as she's just talking—saying what she needs to, expressing her raw emotion and painful truth.

"Can you imagine what it's like to know that the person you dedicated your life to tried to kill you?" she says. "The person who you literally gave up your life for. I've had no life for so long I'm not sure I know how to have one again. The person whose secrets you kept. The person whose work you did. The person whose life you protected. The person whose reputation you defended. *That* person—not an enemy, not a stranger—*that* person tried to kill you. Can you imagine the hurt and humiliation—the shock and disbelief?"

"I know. I'm—"

"I don't think you do."

"You're right. How could I? I just mean . . . Tana, I'm so sorry. I was out of my mind. Truly insane. I'm so sorry."

"It'd be one thing to find out that your hero, your mother figure didn't care for you the way you thought she did. It's another to find out she didn't just want you dead but actually tried to kill you. I'm tellin' you . . . it's the most shocking thing you can ever experience."

Malia is shaking her head, tears streaming down her cheeks. "I know they're just words and they mean nothing compared to what I did, but . . . I'm truly, truly sorry."

"If it weren't for John, I'd be dead right now. Dead. Never married. Never having a child. Never having my own life. Never seeing my own book come out. Never . . . Never getting to do any of the things I wanted to."

"I'm so, so grateful you're still alive. So thankful to John for saving you. I can't even fathom what I was— I really don't even recognize that person at all. I would have sworn I wasn't capable of what I did—not under any circumstances. I don't think I am now. And I didn't then. Even when I did it, it was like I was watching someone else do it."

"Well you were. You are. You aren't just capable of murder. You actually committed it."

"That's true. You're right. I still can't even believe it. I truly can't. But you're right. I'm guilty of murder, of trying to kill the person who wasn't just helping me the most but who was closest to me. Just doesn't seem real."

"But it is. It's very real for me. Too real."

"I've never understood why attempted murder carries a lesser sentence than murder," Malia says. "Both criminals committed the same act. One was successful. One wasn't. But the act was the same. I should be punished as a murderer, not an attempted murderer."

I nod. "I agree," I say, "but that's not the way our imperfect system works. You can't be convicted of a murder you didn't commit."

"So what do I do?" Malia says. "Just confess to attempted murder?"

"We can work with PCPD and the State's Attorney's office on the charges and the confession."

Tana says, "Why aren't you defending yourself, trying to get out of it, negotiating for a lesser sentence?"

"There *is* no defense."

"Doesn't stop most people from making one," Tana says.

"I've felt so guilty, been wanting to confess—really since the moment I did it. Actually started to a few times . . . and in my mind I was convinced I was going to, that I was just working up my nerve. So I was ready to confess even before John confronted me. I just . . . feel . . . so relieved—relieved to be confessing, relieved you're alive. Nothing else matters now. Nothing.

"You don't mind going to prison?"

"Of course *I mind*. But I deserve it. I'm getting off light compared to what I should be getting. And that's all thanks to John. But the truth is . . . I'm so happy you're alive, so relieved I didn't do what my temporarily insane self tried to do that I really don't care about anything else. I would've taken it back the moment I realized I had done it but I couldn't. Except John made it so I could." She turns to me. "You've given me the greatest gift ever—the ability to turn back time and undo, if not my actions, at least the consequences of them. Thank you so much for that."

"Your response lets me know I was right about you," I say.

"I'm nothing but grateful," she says. "You didn't just save her life. You saved mine too."

56

The soft orange-pink aura around the setting sun backlights Lake Julia and the cypress trees at her edges.

It's a few days later. A Saturday. And Anna and I are sitting on our back patio holding hands, watching as Johanna and Taylor play in the early May gloaming gathering over our backyard.

Anna is asking me insightful questions about the case, listening intently as I process what I still need to by thinking about it then giving voice to mysteries too deep to do anything but reflect on.

"You think her sorrow was sincere?" she asks.

"I do," I say.

"That she was as truly repentant as she seemed?"

"I really do."

"Of course, you *are* given to seeing the best in people," she says.

I smile. "Certainly hope so."

She nods. "There are worse things."

In the end, mercy triumphed over judgment and Tana decided she didn't want Malia going to prison for what she had done.

I can only guess at why she didn't. Only Tana knows for sure, and it's possible that not even she really does. But I think it had everything to do with Tana's character, her kind and loving nature, her commitment to the cause and not wanting Malia's destructive behavior to do lasting damage to it, and at least partially because of Malia being such a mother figure to her. What child wants to send her mother to prison—no matter what she has done?

In the end, Malia and I—and even Kevin Pelt—agreed that it was Tana's decision to make.

Instead, Malia went away quietly to focus on public service out of the public eye—something I'm convinced she will do with the fervor and humility of someone doing penance for a great and terrible sin. But not before calling her editor and asking her to publish her new book under Tana's name and to give Tana a contract for the book that Malia had attempted to steal.

The publisher refused, of course, but undaunted, Tana has decided to self-publish both books—which with the effusive praise heaped on them by Malia in both a blurb and an introduction—should prove a successful endeavor.

Tana will never be the speaker or movement leader that Malia was, but I'm betting through her books she becomes something of the conscience of the movement.

I realize as I talk through things with Anna that I never feel like a case is truly over until I am able to do so. Being able to explore the case more deeply while hearing our daughters shriek and squeal as they safely and enthusiastically run and play is a gift that defies description.

"You think she'll stay out of the limelight?" Anna asks. "Not be seduced out of her anonymity by it?"

"I do," I say. "And not just because we could expose what she did if she tries to. I think seeing what she was capable of shook her down to her foundation. But we've established I'm given to seeing the best in people."

"You gave her an extraordinary gift," she says. "To let her carry out a crime like that without actually committing it or suffering the consequences of it . . ."

"Oh, there are consequences."

"You know what I mean."

"Yes," I say. "I do."

"Only Tana owes you more."

"The consequences part of Malia's fate was up to Tana," I say. "That was all her."

"'Course Trevon Fisher owes you a great deal too," she says.

The charges against Trevon Fisher were dropped and he has been taken off administrative leave.

But nobody owes me anything, and nothing I do can make up for what I did to Derek Burrell.

I continue seeing Dave regularly. Alcohol continues to be a non-issue for me—at least for now, but killing Derek Burrell does. And probably always will. As will the wrongful death suit filed against me by his family that continues to drag on and on—and will for the foreseeable future.

Boyd Calhoun was convicted of manslaughter, and his partner, Kenny Floyd who was charged after all and took a plea deal, was charged as an accessory, but both were given extremely lenient sentences.

I will return to work on Monday, both to my full-time position as a sheriff's investigator and my part-time position as a prison chaplain, and I'm looking forward to it—to our lives returning to something resembling normalcy and mundanity.

And that's exactly what it will do—until, on July 22nd, Dave dies suddenly and shockingly of a heart attack, alone in Japan just a few short weeks before he is to return home again.

No crime for me to solve. No culprit to capture. Dave is just cruelly, randomly, unceremoniously dead. In a very short time, Dave has a significant impact on my life, and I now carry a part of him, his wit and wisdom, his insight and compassion, with me, and will as long as I live.

I continue to find the mysteries of life and death, love and meaning, the greatest of all. How can human beings do such inhumane things to one another? Why do the wicked prosper to the extent they do? How can Dave really be dead? How can Reggie and Merrick not be together? How can I love Anna and our girls the way I do without coming apart at the seams?

And how can I know as I sit here holding Anna's hand and watching our wild angels run around in the sweet, soft glow of the setting sun that a category 5 hurricane named Michael will hit us on October 10, 2018, and decimate so much of this place we call home? How can I know that in its aftermath I will face a case that tests the limits of my skills as a detective even as the apocalyptic surroundings test my limits as a human being?

I can't. In this moment I can't know any of that, so I sit in the present moment in the presence of my three girls happy and content and blissfully unaware of the unfolding path before me. And I am grateful to God to be able to do so.

DON'T MISS AND THE SEA BECAME BLOOD

AND THE SEA BECAME BLOOD

Go to www.MichaelLister.com to order your copy now.

The death of elderly loner Emmett Daughtry begins like any other murder investigation for John Jordan, but it ends in a thrilling cat and mouse chase during an existential storm of apocalyptic proportions.

AND THE SEA BECAME BLOOD — the 21st John Jordan Mystery Thriller and Author Michael Lister's response to living through Hurricane Michael, the Cat 5 hurricane that devastated John Jordan's beloved Gulf Coast.

25% of all profits donated directly to Hurricane Michael disaster assistance.

Go to www.MichaelLister.com to order your copy now.

ALSO BY MICHAEL LISTER

Join Michael's Readers' Group and receive 4 FREE Books!

Books by Michael Lister

Sign up for Michael's newsletter at

www.MichaelLister.com and receive a free book.

(John Jordan Novels)

Power in the Blood

Blood of the Lamb

Flesh and Blood

(Special Introduction by Margaret Coel)

The Body and the Blood

Double Exposure

Blood Sacrifice

Rivers to Blood

Burnt Offerings

Innocent Blood

(Special Introduction by Michael Connelly)

Separation Anxiety

Blood Money Blood Moon

Thunder Beach

Blood Cries

A Certain Retribution

Blood Oath

Blood Work

Cold Blood

Blood Betrayal

Blood Shot

Blood Ties

Blood Stone

Blood Trail

Bloodshed

Blue Blood

And the Sea Became Blood

(Jimmy Riley Novels)

The Girl Who Said Goodbye

The Girl in the Grave

The Girl at the End of the Long Dark Night

The Girl Who Cried Blood Tears

The Girl Who Blew Up the World

(Merrick McKnight / Reggie Summers Novels)

Thunder Beach

A Certain Retribution

Blood Oath

Blood Shot

(Remington James Novels)

Double Exposure

(includes intro by Michael Connelly)

Separation Anxiety

Blood Shot

(Sam Michaels / Daniel Davis Novels)

Burnt Offerings

Blood Oath

Cold Blood

Blood Shot

(Love Stories)

Carrie's Gift

(Short Story Collections)

North Florida Noir

Florida Heat Wave

Delta Blues

Another Quiet Night in Desperation

(The Meaning Series)

Meaning Every Moment

The Meaning of Life in Movies